FANG GANG 3

CYN

CONTENTS

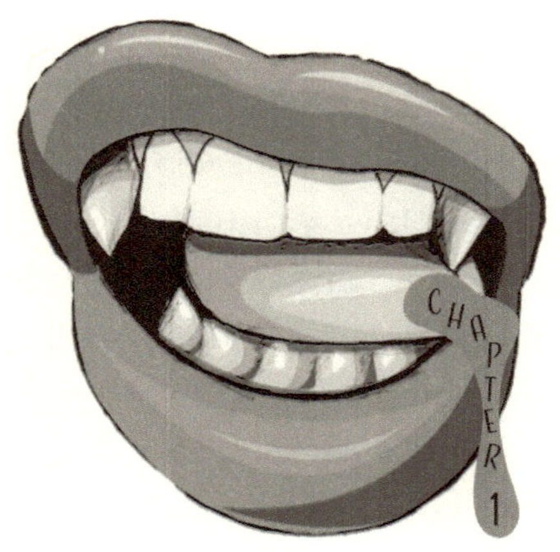

THE MOON SHONE BRIGHTLY, and the stars were clear, giving light to the happenings on Earth. The private cemetery in Salem was where every Bordeaux witch had been buried since the 1800s. Fallon, of course, didn't have any previous head-stones of her own, but she found it interesting to visit Lily's various ones as well as her other coven sisters. She oddly felt comfort in the fact that her sisters were here. It wasn't creepy at all, not even at night. It felt like… home.

That night, it was the celebration of life for Lily Bordeaux. All her coven sisters were in attendance, laughing, smiling, and reminiscing about their coven leader and the lives she lived thus far.

Under different circumstances, Fallon would have been overjoyed to have all her sisters there. She even got to meet some of their husbands, their children, and mini versions of witches she had known in other lifetimes. Magic was truly in the air while the bonfire rose toward the sky and drinks flowed. This was how they did funerals. It was a ritual that took place any time a Bordeaux witch passed, and Fallon used to love funerals because they were more like parties to her. This one, however, felt different. Maybe it was because all she seemed to think about for the past five days was avenging her grandmother's death, or maybe it was because this death seemed to hit her differently. Any time a witch passed, it was hard, no doubt, but Lily's deaths always seemed to hit Fallon harder each time she happened to outlive her twin flame. This time felt personal. She hadn't roamed Earth with Lily in a millennia, and when she finally got her memories back and could really cherish her Lily flower… she was taken away from her.

Fallon was absolutely not okay. Not one bit, but as she watched the party take place around her, the feeling of her heart swelling with love couldn't be ignored. Some of the witches were mingling with the gang, and everyone seemed to be having a good time. Everyone but her.

As she sat in the shadows on a wooden bench watching everyone and plotting her revenge, she felt a tap on her shoulder. She turned slightly to see Julianne, a young witch who was only ten years old in this lifetime and wise beyond her years. Currently, she was technically a third cousin or something like that, but they had lived a previous lifetime together before where Julianne was her aunt, and Fallon was her niece. Julianne went on to live many more lifetimes while Fallon was being punished by the powers that be for creating vampirism, causing the young girl before her to have the soul of a wise old lady.

Fallon forced a smile on her face and tugged on one of Julianne's curls. "Hey, lady bug. What's up?"

Julianne scrunched her face up and said, "Don't do that," before sitting down next to Fallon, who let out a laugh at the child-like tone of her voice in contrast to the grown ass way she spoke.

"Do what, lil girl?"

"Be fake. I know you're angry. I can feel it," Julianne replied.

Fallon nodded. "You aren't wrong."

They sat in silence for a few moments, Julianne kicking her legs back and forth beneath her. Finally, she said, "You're going to see her again, you know?"

Fallon nodded. "I know."

Julianne shook her head. "No… I mean, you'll see her again soon. It won't be long. She is going to be reborn in the next generation."

It was then Fallon remembered one of her coven

sisters mentioning that Julianne was a seer. This time, Fallon's smile was genuine. "You can see that?"

Julianne nodded. "Her spirit is determined to get back to you. She really loves you, you know?"

Tears clouded Fallon's vision, and she clenched her jaw tightly to keep from crying as she nodded. "I know. And I love her. Thanks, lady bug."

Fallon leaned in and hugged Julianne, and the young girl reciprocated before pulling away and saying, "That's what I used to call you. Back when I was your auntie. Why did you steal my nickname?"

Fallon shrugged before tugging on another pigtail. "Because I can."

Julianne rolled her eyes before walking away, leaving Fallon to process the news she dropped on her. While she found comfort that she and Lily would be reunited within the next generation, it did nothing to dull the ache that settled in her heart and the anger simmering just below the surface. Fallon took in some calming breaths so she didn't inadvertently push her emotions out onto everyone else. It was something she had been working on over the past few days, and she was getting better at controlling her gift.

By the time she opened her eyes, Remington was sitting beside her looking out at the crowd of people. Fallon's smile was easy when he was around, and she leaned her head over so it was resting on his shoulder, naturally gravitating toward him.

"I can feel you, my love," Remington murmured as he watched everyone party.

Fallon didn't respond. In fact, she hadn't said much since her grandmother died. She just sat in a silent agony over what happened, not responding to anyone's ploys to cheer her up. Julianne had been the first one to get more than two words out of her all week.

Remington sighed because of her silence and wrapped an arm around her. "You aren't alone, baby. You know your coven's got you, right? So does the gang… and me. We're just waiting on your direction."

She knew that. Everyone was waiting on her. She was at the thick of all this bullshit, and they expected her to act as a leader. Although she understood why… she didn't want to take on that role. She just wanted Maximus and Prima dead and to move the fuck on with her life, but she felt as though killing the king and queen would only cause more responsibility to fall into her lap, and she wasn't sure she was ready for that. That was the only reason she had yet to speak or come up with a solid plan. So… agony it was until she could get her shit together.

Remington knew she wasn't going to respond, so

he simply kissed her forehead before saying, "You need to talk to Kendrick, baby."

Fallon's retort was immediate, and she instantly wished she could take some of the snap out of her tone. "You talk to him."

Remington simply chuckled. "Me and that nigga ain't got shit to talk about, but I think he needs you right now."

Fallon snorted. "And that doesn't bother you?"

Remington pushed a strand of Fallon's ginger hair out of her face and shook his head. "A month ago it would have, but no. That shit don't bother me. I recognize you have a certain type of love for him, but that love don't come close to what we share. I'm at peace with it, baby."

Fallon peered over at him. "And you stand on the fact that y'all don't have shit to talk about?"

Remington stared out at the crowd once again, taking several moments to respond. "That shit is a lost cause. That nigga don't want to hear nothing I have to say."

"You don't know that. You helped save him from y'all's parents. He might be willing to listen," Fallon argued.

"I know what you're doing, my love, and it won't work," Remington replied.

"What?" Fallon asked innocently.

He shook his head. "Stop trying to get the focus off you. I need you to snap out of this funk and help us get to The Guild. We need your help. I feel like you're the only one that can get through to Kendrick, and we need his help to pull this shit off. The Guild will be gunning for us, so we need to be ready."

"I hear you," Fallon replied before standing. "I'll see you back at home."

With that, she teleported, leaving Remington sitting there by himself shaking his head. Fallon was his baby… his heart, but damn if she wasn't hard headed as hell.

Fallon appeared right inside her bedroom at her grandmother's house. She had been making modifications to the house over the past few days. It kept her busy and the others out of her way. She expanded the inside, creating an entire corridor for the gang to each have their own rooms. She also expanded her childhood bedroom and made it more comfortable for her and Remington.

She flopped down on the king sized bed with the black and red comforter. She knew Kendrick was down the hall in his room. She could feel his presence. He had been the only one that didn't attend her grandmother's celebration of life. He had been keeping to himself and hadn't said one word to anyone since they got him back. Fallon recognized that he was suffering, and she wished she could help. She wished it was as simple as a conversation, like her mate suggested, but she knew it wasn't. It was deeper than that, and at the moment, she was also suffering, so instead of going to him and utilizing this time alone to talk, she rolled over on her side and closed her eyes. She hadn't been to sleep in a week, and now was as good of a time as any to get some rest.

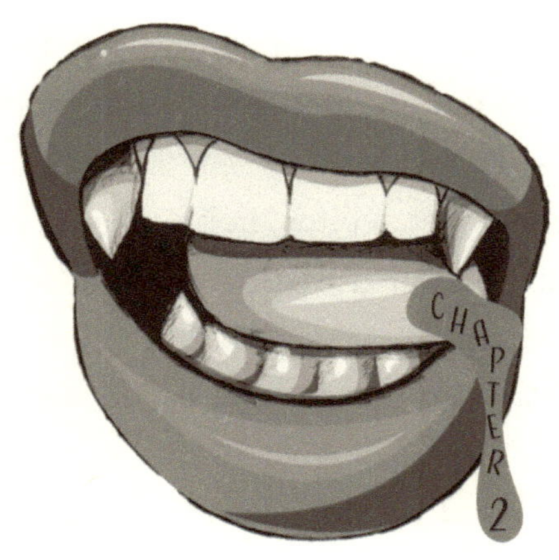

"I'M SICK OF THIS," Papa hissed as he marched into the coven room where Fallon had been reading one of Lily's spell books.

The entire gang followed behind him, minus Kendrick and add Remington instead. Fallon gazed over the top of the book at them all from the over-sized chair she was lounging in. "Sick of what?"

"You," Papa replied as he pointed a black polished finger in her face. "You been moping around here being miserable and a bitch to all of us, and I'm sick of it."

Fallon calmly sat her book down and fought the urge to ease Papa's tension. She could feel it inside her chest, but she wasn't about to give in or let it bother her. She had been trying to learn not to carry everyone's emotions with her. Her gift was not something she wanted to lean on or use to manipulate the people she loved. They were allowed to feel however they wanted, and she had to be okay with that and not allow it to affect her.

"I have not been a bitch, Pablo. You're just in need of attention," Fallon replied as Remington sat on the arm of her chair.

"See!" Papa shrieked. "She called me Pablo! You bitch!"

Tears invaded his eyes, and Fallon sighed heavily as Scarlette pulled Papa back by his shoulders and patted him gently. "I think what he is trying to say is… we miss you, Fal, and we have to start figuring out our next move. It's been a week since we buried Lily. We are thankful for the protection this house provides, but I think we are all becoming a bit stir crazy."

"And what do you want me to do about it?" Fallon asked. She really wasn't trying to be difficult. She was just going through her own process at the moment, and everyone seemed to be upset that it didn't include them.

"Bitch, you act like you're the only one grieving. I loved your grandmother, too!" Papa cried dramatically.

Fallon blinked at him before saying, "You knew her for five minutes."

"And they were the best five minutes I have ever

experienced," Papa replied as he fanned his fake ass tears away.

Fallon rolled her eyes as Remington pulled her into him. "We just want to get a handle on shit, baby. We need your help."

Fallon looked at everyone and shook her head. Before she could say anything, Papa butted in, now completely happy like he wasn't just shedding fake tears seconds ago. "But first, we decided we are going to have a night out."

Fallon looked at them like they were crazy before looking up at Remington. "You agreed to this? Aren't you worried about The Guild?"

He shrugged. "Yeah… but I do think we could use a night out, my love. We'll take extra precaution, and tomorrow we will get to work on figuring out what to do about Maximus and Prima."

Fallon was hesitant. The last thing she wanted was a night out. She preferred spending the night alone in the coven room reading over spells, but she could tell the gang was fed the fuck up with her.

"We're going to get Kendrick to come with us, too. I'm going to talk to his ass next," Axel said.

"I'm surprised you're down for this," Fallon replied as she looked at Axel. He looked stressed and even a little defeated, and Fallon's heart ached a little. She knew how much the gang meant to him, and everyone was doing their own thing. She knew he was hurting behind it and just wanted to get shit back to how it was before. The issue was… it would never be the same again.

He shrugged, and once again, Papa butted in. "Besides… did we forget about this lovely potion you were so kind enough to make me?"

He produced the vial with the cure in it, and Fallon had to admit that she had forgotten about it with everything going on. It surprised her that Papa hadn't used it already.

"You aren't getting out of this, bestie," Scarlette said. "Once we talk to Kendrick, I'll be back for you to help get you ready."

Fallon groaned slightly before leaning back in her chair as she watched Axel, Scarlette, and Papa file out of the room. She looked up at her mate and said, "I guess that's that, huh?"

He chuckled. "Pretty much, my love. Pretty much."

The dimly lit club was the last place both Kendrick and Fallon wanted to be. They sat at the bar looking at the other vamps partying it up. Fallon scanned the room once again, her nerves on high alert and ready to react at the first sign of danger. Finally, she peered over at Kendrick after assuring there was no threat, and she sighed heavily. He didn't look good. He hadn't had a haircut in God knew how long, and she wasn't convinced he had fed or slept, either.

She leaned over to him and said, "Hey."

He glanced at her. "What, Fallon?"

She cringed at that. She knew she hadn't been the most compassionate person over the last couple of weeks, but he wasn't all that approachable, either. They were just two vampires orbiting around each other, trying not to cause destruction in their paths.

"Just checking on you," she mumbled, already regretting that she even tried speaking to him.

He scoffed. "K."

His attitude confused her. Sure, he hadn't been too happy with her the last time they talked when she was packing her things to leave The Lair, but he wasn't being this dickish, either, and because her own emotions were all over the place based on the events from the past few weeks, she served him with the same energy he was giving her. "The fuck is your problem?"

He turned his body toward her with a glare in his eyes. "You're my mothafuckin' problem."

Fallon reared back. "Me? What the fuck did I do to you besides save your goofy ass from your parents?"

She knew she had done a lot more to him, but her emotions were getting the best of her at the moment, and she wasn't thinking rationally.

"Right. Like you didn't break my fuckin' heart. If that nigga ain't bite you, I never would have been held prisoner by my parents."

"How is this my fault, Kendrick?" Fallon asked with tears in her eyes. She felt her emotions expanding, and she had to take a deep breath to reel them in before she cuffed his chin roughly and forced him to look at her. "I had no control over any of that, but if blaming me makes you feel better, do that shit. Hate me if that's what it takes for you to feel better… but I need you to start feeling the fuck better because this ain't it, Kenny."

His eyes softened slightly, and he clenched his jaw tightly. Fallon let her hand fall from his face as he said, "You're one to talk."

Fallon ate that because he was right. She hadn't been doing herself any favors lately, and she knew that. She also knew she needed to have her head on straight in order to dive into this war, but she hadn't been ready to do all that just yet.

She gazed at Kendrick, and her heart ached. She

hated what had become of them. They used to be so in love. He had been her best fucking friend. Her protector. Her everything for so long… she missed him, but she knew things could never be the same between them. Something in him had changed, and it wasn't just their breakup and Remington coming back into his life. She stared at him for a moment before whispering, "What did they do to you?"

Kendrick shook his head before staring down at the glass filled with Hennessy in front of him. After several long seconds he said, "I haven't attempted to turn anyone since Axel… you know how seriously I take that shit. My father… Maximus… he forced me to bite and kill hundreds of people… hundreds, Fallon. I can still hear their screams. I can remember every one of their faces… I—"

Fallon's arms were wrapped around his neck before he could finish. It was no secret that Kendrick was a killer. Everyone in the gang was. Typically, it was in self defense, protection, or whoever it was truly deserved it. He was a savage and ruthless when he needed to be, but Fallon knew there was more than that to him. He had a heart, and it seemed as though his parents had tried to tarnish that goodness that was still left in him.

After a moment, Kendrick's arms wrapped around Fallon, and he squeezed her tightly. They stayed that way for several moments before Kendrick said, "I miss this. I miss us. I miss who I used to be."

Fallon pulled away and looked up at him. She reached up and patted his cheek lovingly. "You're still you."

He shook his head. "I feel like they really fucked with my mind, Fal. They had me doing shit—"

"Hey, you don't have to talk about it unless you want to."

He nodded. "Thank you. I know I been pretty useless around here. I'm just so fuckin' mad… everything has been taken from me."

Fallon sat back in her chair and pondered what she was about to say. A small ache filled her heart, but she knew it was the most selfless thing she could do, and if anyone deserved it, it was Kendrick. "Tell you what… when you're ready, start dating again—"

"What? No—"

Fallon held her hand up. "Just listen. Start dating when you're ready, and when the next blue moon hits in a few years, if you've found a woman you love and can trust, I'll give you the cure for vampire bites."

His eyes widened. "You figured out the cure?"

Fallon realized he hadn't been around for that conversation with the gang, so she smiled sheepishly and said, "Yeah."

He stared at her with that signature crooked smile on his face for a moment before saying, "I'm proud of you, Beauty. I know how much that shit meant to you."

She nodded. "I'm only sorry it couldn't be used how we intended it."

They let the weight of that statement sit between them before Kendrick replied, "Me too."

As always, Papa interrupted a heavy moment when he walked by with a middle aged Black man and Remington at his heels. He sloppily threw his arm over Fallon's shoulders and swayed slightly. "Fal, why didn't you tell me your mans was such a great wing man?"

Fallon cringed and glanced at Kendrick, who turned around in his seat, facing away from them and retreating back into his own world.

Damnit, Pablo, she thought, but she knew it was too late. She could feel the tension building up around Kendrick once again, and she sighed. Silently, she sent a little burst of calm toward him, careful not to over-do it or send it out to anyone else. She had been working on sending energy out in small, directed doses, and when Kendrick turned toward her and gave her a slight nod, she knew it worked. She was glad he wasn't upset. It was only her way of showing him some support in the only form of comfort she could offer him.

Finally, she gave her attention to Remington and asked, "Where are Scarlette and Axel?"

"Last I saw, they were getting their mack on and trying to bring some humans home tonight."

He shrugged as he helped balance Papa, who poked Fallon in the forehead and said, "We're all horny, missy. We been cooped up entirely too long."

Fallon snorted. "Whatever, Pablo."

"You're going to have enough of calling me by my government," he slurred. "Anyway, you're being rude. This here is Calvin. He's very interested in becoming a vampire."

Fallon's eyes grew wide as they shifted over to Remington, searching for an explanation. Once again, he shrugged and said, "There really is no controlling him, my love. You know that."

"He's drunk," Calvin said with a laugh. "But he's kind of adorable. Who doesn't love a man with a great imagination?"

He looked at Papa with a light in his eyes, amused by the younger looking man and not knowing how serious this shit truly was. Calvin seemed to be a bit tipsy as well as he swayed on his feet and took a drink from the glass in his hand. Fallon shook her head incredulously at the pair before grabbing Papa by his arm. "Okay, Papa. Time to go home."

He pulled away from her, stumbling slightly. "No! Calvin's wish is my command."

Before anyone coud stop him, Papa was behind Calvin and biting his neck.

"No!" Fallon shouted, and she refrained from putting vamp speed in her run as she made her way to Papa, not wanting to cause a scene. She swiftly looked around before tugging Papa and Calvin into a dark corner and teleporting them back to her grandmother's. Calvin fell to his knees once they landed in the living room, and Papa was right behind him, his mouth still locked on the man's neck. Fallon wanted to curse his ass out, but she would wait until she got back. In a blink, she was back in the bar in an empty bathroom stall. She quickly made her way out of the bathroom and toward Remington, who was now sitting next to Kendrick. They were silent and looking out into the crowd of people. When Fallon stalked over to them, both their eyes lifted to watch her, and her heart stalled for a moment. It was the first time she saw them in a setting not at each other's throats. They probably didn't even realize it, but the sight of them together was powerful. It made tears come to her eyes because she could see how close they had once been, and she wanted that for them again. They looked so much alike, it almost made her uncomfortable as she took the last few steps toward them. Remington stood and gathered her in his arms. Fallon watched as Kendrick turned away, and she knew the moment of what a normal relationship between the brothers could look like was gone. Remington pulled away and grinned down at her. "How pissed are you?"

"Oh! That dumb nigga is going to hear my mouth when we get back. Believe that!" Fallon spat. "Come on, let's get home."

Kendrick stood and made his way out of the bar without a word. Remington leaned down and whispered in Fallon's ear. "I'll get Scarlette and Axel. Meet you out front."

Fallon nodded before making her way out of the bar where everyone's bikes were parked. After much arguing and deliberating, the gang made the hasty decision to go to the old lair and grab a few things. Fallon acted as transport and teleported them and all their shit back to the new lair, also known as Lily's house. They grabbed the important things, including their bikes and cars, and left everything else for the next person to profit off.

It had been awhile since The Fang Gang rode their bikes, and tonight, they showed the fuck out. Fallon stepped outside in time to see Kendrick kick-start his bike and take off. Worry filled her because they were technically still at war with The Guild, but she knew there was no use trying to talk sense into him. She simply said a protection prayer to the powers that be before turning her attention to the remaining motorcycles in the parking lot. She sighed heavily. "Fuckin' Papa."

She had rode on the back of Remington's bike on the way there since she never drove a bike herself. She always rode with someone else, so Papa's glittery purple Ducati was right in the middle of Remington's sleek Black BMW bike and Scarlette's dark red Ducati. Just as the rest of the gang came out of the bar, Fallon decided she would ride Papa's bike back to The Lair instead of teleporting it. She was a vampire now, and if she crashed, she wouldn't break. A grin spread across her face as she thought about crashing. "It would serve him right for the shit he pulled."

"What was that, my love?" Remington asked, coming up behind her.

"Nothing," Fallon replied sweetly.

"Why are we leaving?" Scarlette asked, and Fallon could tell her girl was feeling good. Not only that, she had some human nigga standing behind her and grabbing at her waist. Her girl was sure enough ready to feed and get fucked. Axel had a little Latina girl at his side. She was obviously drunk and hanging all over him. Fallon chuckled at the twins. They were definitely more alike than not.

"Because your friend decided to create his mate… right at the bar in front of all these… people," Fallon replied, careful about what she said in front of the humans.

Axel chuckled as he shook his head, and Scarlette threw her hands up in the air. "Can't take his ass anywhere."

"Say that again," Fallon replied before mounting Papa's bike and starting it.

Remington walked over to her, amused. "You sure you can handle this thing, mama?"

"Nope." She grinned, and he chuckled before mounting his bike.

Scarlette and Axel, along with thier humans, followed suit. They got in formation and took off. Driving the bike was exhilarating to Fallon, and she immediately knew she wanted one for herself. Her reflexes and agility was top tier now that she was a vampire, and once she got the hang of the gears, she was able to keep up with the rest of the gang.

By the time they made it back to The Lair, Fallon felt completely refreshed. She hated to admit it, but her friends had been right. She really did need this night out. Furthermore, she needed that talk with

Kendrick. It was the first step toward healing, and she was grateful it had been taken.

As Fallon got off the bike, she noticed Kendrick's bike was already there, and she said a quiet, "Thank you," as she looked up at the sky.

The gang made their way into the house, and they all stopped in their tracks when they made it to the living room where Calvin and Papa were making out.

"Well, I'll be damned," Scarlette said.

"That was fast," Axel chimed in, referring to the amount of time it took Calvin to turn.

Remington walked up behind Fallon and grabbed her from behind, resting his chin on her shoulder. "My baby is a genius."

Fallon's smile grew because she realized her potion had worked. "Guess we have a new member to welcome to the gang."

Papa finally pulled away from Calvin with happy tears staining his cheeks. Calvin flashed his fangs, and Papa grabbed his mate's face and laughed joyously. "Someone's hungry."

Scarlette pushed the guy she had with her forward. "Here, Papa. Take him. My gift to you. Congrats, baby."

He squealed in excitement as the gang filed out of the living room, leaving the confused human in the hands of Papa and Calvin. As Fallon ascended the stairs, she yelled, "Take that shit into your room, Papa!"

"Si, mami!" he replied just before she heard Calvin bite the human's neck.

There was never a dull moment with these vamps.

FALLON ALLOWED a couple of days to go by so Papa and Calvin could get acquainted so and she could direct her energy into more productive thoughts. She was still hurt and angry, but it was time for her to get the fuck up and do something. Things between her and the gang had been better since she was less moody and more open to talking to them. Finally, she felt it was time to put a plan in motion. Something in her gut had been bothering her, and she wanted to share it with everyone.

It was early, and everyone was ducked off in their own worlds, leaving room for Fallon to get a big breakfast started. On her way to the kitchen, she paused in the living room where Remington was playing the piano. There hadn't originally been one there, but Remington had one delivered the day before, and as she stopped to listen, she wondered if there was anything he couldn't do.

"You just gonna stand there, or are you going to come give me a kiss?" Remington asked with his back still turned to her, never missing a key.

She chuckled and sauntered over to him. He turned his head, and they shared a kiss. Still, he didn't miss a beat as his fingers tapped along the keys, creating a sweet melody.

"You cease to amaze me," Fallon said.

Remington simply winked and continued to play as Fallon continued on her way to the kitchen. She hadn't realized Scarlette was already in there, and Fallon's smile was immediate. Scarlette, who was sipping on a cup of coffee, wrinkled her nose. "So she smiles?"

Fallon grabbed an oven mitt that was sitting on the counter and threw it at her best friend, aiming for her head. Scarlette caught it effortlessly and nonchalantly placed it on the counter next to her coffee mug. Fallon flopped down into the bar stool sitting at the island and sighed. "Okay, I know I was a bit of an ass for a few weeks, but I was really going through it."

Scarlette shrugged. "I can imagine. I truly don't envy you. Your wedding got crashed, you got mated to your groom's brother, you turned into a vampire against your will, you remembered you were the one to create vampirism, you reunited with your grandmother, you had to relearn to control your powers, The Guild is hunting you, your ex was captured by them and tortured, and when you tried to save him your grandmother died. Yeah… you don't need to apologize." Fallon cringed at the long list of shit Scarlette just ticked off like she was reporting the weather, but her bestie continued talking, saving Fallon from having to respond. "I just missed you is all. Since you turned, I haven't really gotten any BFF time."

Fallon stood from the stool and slinked over to Scarlette, wrapping her arms around her shoulders and pulling her in for a hug. Scarlette reciprocated before the two pulled apart and Fallon asked, "Want to know the good thing about all this?"

"What?" Scarlette asked.

"We have an eternity for BFF time," Fallon replied.

Scarlette's smile was dazzling as she processed what Fallon said before she asked, "What are you about to do?"

"I was going to make breakfast," Fallon admitted as she walked over to the refrigerator and opened it.

"You're in luck. I placed a grocery order last night, and they were delivered about an hour ago. Need help?"

Fallon turned back around to face Scarlette and said, "I would love that."

"Damn, that was good, baby," Remington said as he leaned back in his chair and rubbed his stomach.

Fallon giggled, happy that she was starting to feel a sense of normalcy again. "Scarlette helped."

"Both of y'all did ya thang," Papa announced before belching.

Calvin shook his head and said, "Excuse my mate."

"Y'all hear that?" Papa asked, damn near on the verge of tears. "His *mate*."

Nobody replied to his dramatic ass, but everyone was happy as hell for Papa. He was newly in love and finally found his mate. The great thing about Calvin was he was a romantic mate for Papa. The hopeless romantic finally got what he wanted and had been on cloud nine ever since.

"Calvin, how are you adjusting?" Fallon asked, genuinely curious. She knew how overwhelming turning could be, especially since Calvin didn't know vampires were a real thing until he turned, so she wanted to make sure he was comfortable. He was family now, after all.

Calvin smiled, and Fallon had to admit, she understood why Papa was so smitten with him. Calvin was a charmer. He was older than the rest of them, in human years, anyway, with salt and pepper hair and perfectly straight teeth. His skin was a smooth Hershey brown, and he used to wear glasses. Now, his brown eyes had the ability to see without them.

"Honestly, it's a lot to take in. The morning after I turned, I woke up sure I had just had a bad dream. When I realized it was very much real, I kind of freaked out."

"We heard you," Scarlette said matter of factly before sipping from her fresh mug of coffee.

Fallon snickered because it was true. Calvin completely freaked out, and Papa had to calm his ass down and explain everything to him with sober minds. They spent a lot of time together after that, getting to know each other and getting Calvin acquainted with being a vampire. That day was the first time anyone had really seen the pair.

Calvin nodded sheepishly. "Sorry about that. It's just—"

"It's a lot to take in. I get it," Fallon finished for him.

He nodded, thankful that someone understood, before Papa voiced his opinion. "I think he's doing great."

The two nuzzled into each other, and Axel, who had been relatively quiet during dinner, spoke up. "Thanks for breakfast, y'all."

"Welcome, bro," Scarlette replied.

"Don't stray too far. I want to have a meeting in a few once I get the kitchen cleaned," Fallon called after him.

He lifted his hand in acknowledgement before he left the room, carrying his dirty dishes. Remington lifted from the table and grabbed his and Fallon's dishes. "Don't worry, love. I'll clean up."

She smiled up at him, but before she could respond, Papa said, "Yeah, Romeo here's got it."

And before anyone could say shit, Papa grabbed Calvin's hand and pulled him up, rushing him out of the room.

"You ain't shit," Scarlette called after them. "I'll help, Remington."

"Nah, I got it," he replied as he continued clearing dishes.

Fallon stood. "I'll leave y'all to fight over that. I'm going to see if I can coax Kendrick into sitting in on this meeting with us."

"Good luck," Scarlette replied dryly. Kendrick

had still been keeping to himself, but Fallon figured he would more than likely be in on whatever planning that had to do with taking his parents down.

Remington stopped what he was doing and placed a kiss on her forehead. "We'll be ready when you are."

Fallon offered him a small smile before she left the kitchen.

Once she made it upstairs, she inhaled deeply before knocking. A second later, she heard Kendrick say, "Go away."

Fallon ignored him and opened the door anyway, poking her head inside. "Hey."

"What, Fallon?" he asked. He was sitting on his bed scrolling on his phone. He didn't even look up from his phone when he spoke.

"I wanted to have a meeting. I think it's time we put a plan in place—"

"I'll be down in a minute," Kendrick replied, completely cutting her off.

Fallon lingered in the doorway for a moment before stepping further inside the room. She stopped just in front of Kendrick and waited patiently for him to look at her. When he finally did, she asked, "How can I help?"

He took a moment before he responded. "Honestly, Fallon… once all this shit blows over, I'm going to need some time alone. That's what will help. To be away from you."

Fallon's heart shattered at that, but she understood. She couldn't blame him at all, but she would miss him. That was a fact. She reached out and squeezed his shoulder. "Whatever you need."

She didn't wait for him to respond before she turned and left the room, her heart aching. She hated the place she and Kendrick were in, but she had to respect his process and what he was going through. She and Remington had thrown him a huge curveball, and she knew she couldn't be any more selfish than she already had been with him, so she tucked away her feelings and focused on what was to come.

Once she got back downstairs, she sat in the living room and made herself comfortable on the couch before she softly said, "I'm ready when y'all are."

She knew everyone in the house could hear her, and one by one, they came trickling into the room a few minutes later. The last one in was Remington, who sat next to Fallon and placed his arm around her shoulders. She cleared her throat, and then prepared herself to tell them what had been on her mind the past few days.

"I'll just get straight to the point. I know we need to figure out what we are going to do about The

Guild so we can all start living our lives normally again. I can't explain it other than to say it's a witch's intuition… but I've has this nagging feeling that I need to go back to where all this shit started."

It was quiet for a moment before Axel spoke up. "You mean back to the old lair?"

Fallon shook her head and opened her mouth to respond, but Kendrick beat her to it. "New Netherland."

"New Amsterdam," Remington piggybacked off his brother.

Fallon nodded and clarified. "Which is now New York."

It was silent for a moment before Papa said, "Shit, when do we leave?"

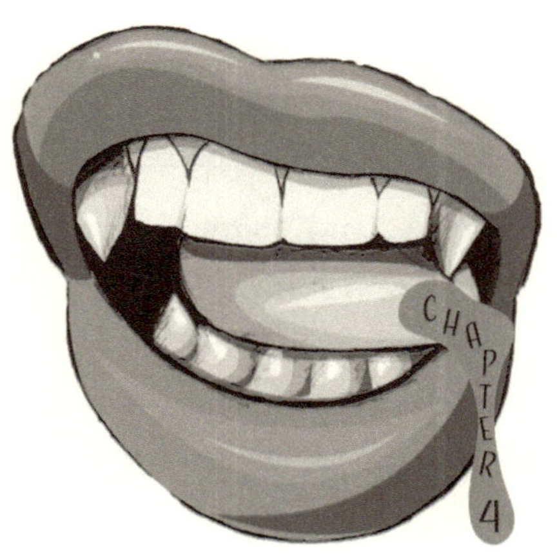

THE COVEN ROOM served many purposes. For Fallon, it had become a sanctuary. It was a place where peace resided and magic could be felt in every crevice. At the moment, though, it served as a conference room. She hadn't spoken to her coven since Lily's funeral, and before that, she hadn't spoken to them since Lily died. Communication with them was not something she wanted at the moment because she knew what they expected of her, and she was not ready. She was also a little afraid to face them because Lily had not been the only coven sister to die after their attack on The Guild. She felt guilty, even though she knew everyone had a say in if they wanted to help or not. Still, she couldn't help but feel this was her mess.

Fallon waited patiently for her sisters to hop on the Zoom call. It was amusing to her how they chose to run their meetings. They were witches… they could be teleporting all over the world and having these meetings, but the vampires really had them secluded, in hiding, and using Zoom like they were on a work call or some shit.

One by one, her coven sisters appeared on the screen. They each greeted her and then each other. Soon, everyone was logged on and had their attention on Fallon, since she was the one who called the meeting. She cleared her throat, suddenly nervous for some reason. She never had an issue with being in control before, but she knew the weight of what both her coven and the gang wanted from her, and she still wasn't anywhere near ready for that responsibility. Still, she understood that shit was being pushed off on her, and she would be lying if she said she wasn't at least intrigued to see what it would be like to be in a position of power on both the witch's end and the vampire's end. She had led her coven before. That part was easy. It was the bridging the gap between other covens and vampires outside of the gang that was troublesome for her. She didn't now those people nor what trauma they had been through at the hands of each other. That was a big ass job, but luckily, that wasn't the point of the meeting that day, so Fallon took a deep breath and spoke. "I've already spoke with my vampire family earlier, and we have decided to go to New York where this all began. I know Lily…"

Fallon cleared her throat at the mention of her grandmother. She hated that she was taking Lily's passing so hard. That wasn't how witch's responded to death. She shook it off and took a deep breath before continuing. "I know Lily told you all the story of my previous lifetime. My intuition is telling me to go back to New York and find our old settlement."

"Why do you think that is?" Lidia, one of the eldest witches of this lifetime chimed in and asked.

Fallon shrugged. "I wish I could tell you. It's as if there is something pushing me toward going there. I understand that the focus is on taking down The Guild. I know we each lost a lot a couple of weeks ago, and after taking some time to process, I can assure you my priority is to kill the king and queen… I just feel as though I have to do this first."

Fallon knew it seemed irrational, but her gut wouldn't allow her to move on with anything that had to do with The Guild until she visited New York. She hadn't been there since her previous life, and she felt she was missing something.

"Is it too cold for you to go there this time of year?" Samiyah asked.

Fallon shook her head. "I checked the weather,

and according to the gang, we will be fine. It is starting to get cold, but not enough to do damage."

A few people nodded, and Fallon was relieved they seemed to be so understanding, but then again, of course they would be. She should have known, as witch's, they would understand how strong the will of an intuition could be. It was funny because warlocks didn't have it this bad. At least, not that she could remember. There were no warlocks within her coven, unless they were married in within a lifetime. Her coven was all female, but that was not the case for all covens. The sayings about the female intuition derived from witches. Since the beginning of time, witches had stronger intuition than warlocks. It was like the powers that be gave witches their own super power, and it was an unofficial law to follow it, no matter what, because it was normally right or would lead a witch to where she needed to be.

After a few moments of silence, Samiyah spoke up again and asked, "After that, can we gather some sisters to do a locator spell on The Guild so we can take them down once and for all and you can take over?"

Fallon cringed. Doing a locator spell was fine. She was sure The Guild wasn't at their home in Jamaica anymore after they infiltrated it. Locator spells took a lot of power, so a minimum of five coven sisters would need to be in attendance for that. That was all fine… it was the last part of Samiyah's statement that caused Fallon to cringe.

She sighed heavily and said, "I'm still not sure I'm the best person—"

"You are!" A small voice piped up, and Julianne popped up on the screen, sitting in her mother, Claudia's, lap.

"Girl, I told you if you wanted to join this meeting, you would have to sit still and be quiet," Claudia chastised.

"Sorry, Mama, but I've seen it… Fallon is going to rule over the vampires and the witches."

It was silent for a moment before Samiyah's face filled the screen again. "Well.. there you have it, Fal. You gonna stop fighting it now?"

Fallon clenched her jaw. She loved Julianne, but she wished she didn't know that piece of information. Not now, at least.

"Listen… let me make this trip tomorrow, and while I'm doing that, you all can start a locator spell on the king and queen to keep tabs on them so we can figure out a plan of attack. I'll touch base tomorrow, but text or call if you need anything."

Fallon didn't wait for responses. She ended the call and sat back in the chair she was occupying. The weight of the world seemed to rest on her shoulders, and suddenly, she was exhausted. She dragged herself out of the chair and through the house, realizing she needed to catch a couple of hours of sleep before they teleported to New York tomorrow, because she had absolutely no idea what was in store for her when they got there.

A FEW HOURS was truly all it took. Fallon's eyes fluttered open, and all her senses tuned back into the world. She heard footsteps coming toward her bedroom door, and before it even opened, she knew it was Remington. Not only by the sound of his steps but because any time they weren't in each other's arms, she felt as though there was a string connecting their hearts, and it pulled harder and became more taut the father away from each other they were. When the door opened, she could feel that invisible string loosen, and she felt she could breathe easier.

As soon as Remington's eyes landed on his mate, he dashed over to her and was in bed lying beside her in one second flat. His hand rested on her cheek before he spoke. "Hey, sleepyhead. I was coming to see if you were up yet."

"What time is it?" Fallon asked.

Remington pulled his phone out of his hoodie pocket before glancing at it and responding, "A little past eleven."

It was still evening time, and Fallon had slept for three hours. She felt refreshed and more prepared to take on what felt like the world. She stretched a little before asking, "What's everyone else up to?"

He shrugged. "Ducked off in their own rooms."

Fallon nodded before a mischievous grin spread across her face. "What do you propose we do all night?"

Fallon never fully understood how much time she spent sleeping as a human. It wasn't like she slept all day every day, but as a vampire and not needing to sleep nearly as much, it made Fallon realize how much time was truly in a day because it was now hers to do as she pleased. With school being put all the way on the back burner for her at the moment, she often found herself bored or in deep contemplation about one thing or another. She now understood why the vampires she met seemed to be so intense. They had nothing but time on their hands to figure the world out and sit with their thoughts.

Remington pulled her closer and nuzzled her neck, using his fangs to nip at her skin there. "I can think of a few things."

"Show me," Fallon purred. She woke up hot and

ready. Sex had been the last thing on her mind lately, and her mood swings weren't making it any better, but she felt well rested and in need of a release only Remington could give her.

Remington wasted no time slipping his shirt over his head and doing the same to Fallon's shirt while she kissed on his chest.

"I love you," she breathed.

Remington stopped tugging his pants down, and he stared into her eyes for a moment before leaning in and kissing her sensually on her plump lips. "I love you too, my love."

"For an eternity," she replied.

"And more," he concluded before he said, "Let's see how good this soundproof spell is."

Fallon giggled as she pulled off her biker shorts. She had put a soundproofing spell on all the bedrooms. She knew they were all appreciative, and she couldn't imagine having this super sonic hearing and living without soundproof bedrooms. She didn't want to hear what her roommates were doing, and she damn sure didn't want them to hear her, either.

Fallon pulled Remington to her by his collar and whispered, "Make me scream, daddy."

Remington's dick was already on brick, but the shit got even harden when he heard her words.

"Yeah, aight. Keep that same energy, love. Ain't no tappin' out, either."

"I wouldn't think of it," Fallon challenged, and at that, their banter was cut short when Remington flipped Fallon over, pulled her ass up and pressed down on her upper back. She couldn't get a word out before his face was in her pussy, slurping it from behind like he hadn't eaten all damn day.

"Fuck… Remy," she moaned before stuffing her face into the nearest pillow.

Remington stopped what he was doing, reached around Fallon, and snatched the pillow from under her. "Nah, love. Let me hear you."

He didn't give her a chance to respond before he dove back in. Fallon relaxed her upper body into the soft mattress as she arched her ass even higher, twerking a little bit on Remington's tongue.

He gripped her ass and sucked gently on her clit for several long moments before he inserted one of his fingers into her pussy and used his thumb to rub gentle circles around her asshole. That was all it took for Fallon's juices to squirt out, and Remington didn't stop until she completely folded into the mattress. He bit her ass, using his fangs to pierce her skin. She barely flinched as he made his way back up to her and kissed her cheek. Fallon sent out a wave of gratitude toward him, and he chuckled. "Getting the hang of your gift, huh?"

"And is," Fallon mumbled.

Remington slapped her ass. "Uh uh… get yo' ass up, love. My dick is still hard."

To make his point, he held his throbbing dick in his hand, and Fallon chuckled. "I got you, daddy."

"Show me," he replied, lying back and placing his hands behind his head.

Fallon got up to her knees and leveled her face to his dick, tooting her ass back up in the air.

"Mmm," she moaned just before licking the tip of his dick.

Remington bit his bottom lip and watched his girl get to work. She took his entire dick into her mouth and suctioned her lips around him, causing him to groan and grab a fistful of her hair. "Fuck, Fallon."

She then used both her hands to massage his dick as she bobbed her head up and down. Remington loved to watch her work, so he did just that… he enjoyed the view, but after a few minutes, he had to stop her because no way was he about to bust without diving into that dripping pussy she had between her legs. He reached over and tapped her on her ass before saying, "Raise up, love."

Fallon did as she was told, and Remington was

behind her, grabbing her waist, within half a second. He pushed into her, and they both groaned, loving the feeling of being in each other's essence in this way.

Fallon pushed out her hot and bothered emotions, and Remington chuckled once again. "That's how it is?"

"Uh huh," Fallon replied as she focused on the rhythm he was beating her pussy up to.

He moved her hair away from her ear before leaning over and saying, "Bet."

His rhythm picked up, and Fallon moaned loudly. "Fuck, baby."

"Say my name, love," Remington demanded as he tapped into her guts, rearranging them and shit.

"Remy," she breathed before she threw her ass back, matching his pace.

They made love like that for several moments, keeping up the pace and filling each other with passion and need before Fallon pulled away and turned quickly, pushing him on his back and mounting him all within two seconds. She slid down on his dick slowly and then rocked to the sensual beat in her head. Remington reached up and squeezed her nipples, causing Fallon's head to fall back.

"I'm about to cum, baby," Fallon breathed as her slow wind picked up into a more feverish rhythm.

"Get that shit, love," Remington replied before slapping her ass so hard the sound rippled off the walls and caused Fallon to cry out. A moment later, she was cumming hard. Remington could feel her muscles contracting around him, and he flipped her over so he was on top, keeping up with the pace and looking into her pretty face while she came all over him.

When she was finished, he allowed his nut to build, and he pulled out last second so his seed spilled onto her stomach.

"Fuck," he said before jumping up and going to the connecting bathroom.

A second later, he came back with two wet rags. He cleaned Fallon's stomach with one and used the other to clean himself off. He discarded the rags before climbing back in bed with her. She rested her head on his shoulder and said, "I needed that."

"I know," he replied, gently tracing her nipple with his pointer finger.

Fallon sighed lovingly. She could feel the heat between them turning back up again, but she wanted to make one thing clear. "I'll give you a few more rounds, love, but there is something else I need for us to do before we leave in the morning."

Remington bit her nipple, causing her back to arch, before he asked, "Like what?"

"I'll tell you after you make me cum again," she replied, her breath already becoming unsteady again.

He chuckled. "It's your world, my love."

Fallon bit her bottom lip and enjoyed everything Remington was offering her. She sure as fuck needed this to clear her mind, and she was glad Remington was more than willing to give it.

A FEW HOURS PASSED, and Fallon and Remington had finally come up for air. They showered and threw on some clothes before Fallon sat Remington down and had a talk with him. It was a talk he didn't much care for, but Fallon being Fallon… she couldn't find a single fuck to give.

Currently, they were walking down the dark hallway she created for the gang, whispering to one another and bickering about what they were about to do. Fallon stopped in her tracks and turned around suddenly, but Remington's reflexes were quick enough to stop himself from bumping into her. His reflexes were not quick enough to stop Fallon from shoving him against the wall and strong-arming him so he was stuck there, however. Remington clenched his jaw and glared at his mate. Fallon, on the other hand, was as cool as a cucumber. She met Remington's gaze before murmuring, "This is happening, love. Accept it."

"Fal—"

"Aht!" she snapped before putting a finger to his lips. "Not another word, Remy."

Quick as lightning, he bit her finger, and Fallon winced at the sharp pain, but she didn't budge. "I can get with the rough shit, baby."

Remington chuckled before blowing out a frustrated breath. Fallon watched him for a couple of seconds before asking, "You good now?"

Remington simply stared at her with a blank expression, and she took that as confirmation to continue on her mission. She softly pecked his lips before moving away and further down the hallway. When she stopped outside Kendrick's door, she knocked and waited patiently for him to answer.

When he did, she could tell he had been asleep. His dreads were all over the place at the top of his head and in dire need of being redone, and his eyes looked sleepy as he gazed at her. "What up, Fallon?"

She had to refrain from cringing at the formal way he spoke to her. Not too long ago, their words were filled with nothing but love. She wished there could be a way to get back to that, just on a different level. If nothing else, she truly missed her best friend, but she knew Kendrick hated being stuffed inside that box, so she didn't push it. She was convinced time was all they needed, and she would wait it out for as long as she had to. When it came to the two brothers, on the other hand, enough time had passed. It was time to nip this shit in the bud sooner rather than later.

"Can we talk?" she asked, shifting from foot to foot, suddenly nervous about how this would all go down.

Kendrick glanced over Fallon's head and saw Remington, and his jaw set. "No."

He tried closing the door, but Fallon's hand snapped out and caught it, holding it in place. Kendrick looked at her like she was crazy, but Fallon wasn't about to back down. "Kenny… please."

His eyes softened slightly at the nickname she used to call him, and he sighed heavily. "Fine."

Fallon's smile was triumphant as she motioned for Kendrick to follow her. She passed Remington up, knowing his ass would follow her to the end of the Earth. The two brothers followed her into the living room, and they made themselves comfortable. Kendrick sat in a chair, and Remington sat on the couch across from his brother. Fallon opted to sit in the middle on the ottomen between them. She looked back and forth between them, and neither of them were looking at her or each other. Instead, they were looking at shit around the living room as if they had never been in there before.

Fallon cleared her throat and said, "Y'all need to talk and hash this shit out."

"It ain't that simple, Fallon," Kendrick replied, preparing to stand up, but she reached out and grabbed his wrist.

"Sit," she demanded, and she was tempted to push out some calming feelings, but she refrained. If this shit was going to happen, then it needed to be authentic… not fueled by her gift.

Kendrick snatched his wrist away from her, but he sat down. Once Fallon was satisfied that she had both their attention, she looked between the two and said, "Look… in the past few weeks I've learned that family is everything. Kendrick, you know I haven't always felt that way. Since my grandma and I fell out I had a distorted view of family. I was ignorant because I wasn't seeing the full picture, and that caused me to miss out on a full lifetime with her. I want you two to learn from me… please… just—"

"I don't see what the big deal is, Fallon. Lily is going to be re-born, and you're immortal now. Y'all will see each other again," Kendrick snapped.

Fallon flinched at his words. He wasn't wrong, but it didn't mean what she was saying was wrong, either. She looked at Remington with sad eyes, and said, "Remy…"

"I'm allowed to talk now?" he asked coolly.

"Huh?" she asked, confused.

"You told me not to say another word upstairs—"

"Oh for fuck's sake! I can't with you two," Fallon cried as she put her head in her hands and let out a sharp breath.

Remington chuckled before pulling her hands away from her face and pinching her chin. "Sorry, love. I hate to admit it, but I agree with Kendrick on this one."

Fallon shook out of his grasp and looked back at Kendrick. Her heart was split. The love she had for Kendrick may have shifted, but she still loved him and wanted what was best for him. She didn't want him to become a loner like Remington had been all those years. She looked back at Remington with sad eyes because she knew how much his family dynamic tortured him. These two men were hard headed as hell, but she had a stronger will than both of them combined, so she crossed her arms and stared straight ahead.

Both men groaned. They each knew her well enough to know she was about to get her way. She was as stubborn as they came, and they knew there was no way getting around this. Remington, being more willing to oblige his mate, initiated the conversation. He leaned forward with his elbows to his knees and cleared his throat. "Look, nigga. I know we don't fuck wit' each other, and that's alright with me—"

"If you're going to do this, do it right and say how you really feel," Fallon snapped, cutting him off.

Remington looked at her incredulously before wiping a hand down his face. Kendrick shook his head and said, "Fallon, this shit ain't going to work. I don't want to hear anything he has to say—"

"Why?" Fallon asked, cutting him off as well. She was going to stay in control of this conversation, even if it killed her. She looked over at Remington and asked, "And why can't you be honest about your feelings? You know just as well as I do that deep down, not having a relationship with your brother is killing you."

Remington's jaw tightened. At that moment, he could have catapulted Fallon across the room because it was not her place to tell Kendrick that shit. It was something they barely talked about. His demeanor hardened, and this time, he stood up to leave, but Fallon was quicker. "Sit down, Remy."

He shook his head. "Nah."

When he tried side-stepping her, Fallon followed,

blocking his path. "You can't keep running away from this."

"Says who?" he bellowed. "You?"

Fallon saw the anger in his eyes, but she knew it wasn't truly aimed at her. She didn't flinch at his glare or his outburst. Instead, she reached her hand up and caressed his cheek softly, only for a second because she didn't want to do too much in front of Kendrick, before she murmured, "Yes."

Kendrick sighed heavily behind them and said, "Man, Remington, let's just get this shit over with. We both know she ain't going to let this go."

Remington's nostrils flared, but he continued to stare down at Fallon, who kept her eyes on him, while she spoke to Kendrick. "Kendrick, is there anything you want to say to your brother?"

Both of the scoffed, but Fallon waited patiently. After a moment, Kendrick replied, "Yeah, actually." He walked over to Fallon and Remington, standing just behind Fallon and looking at Remington over her head. Remington kept his eyes on Fallon, and his jaw clenched and unclenched repeatedly. "Why did you have to come back and fuck shit up for me once again? All you've every done is turned my life upside down. What the fuck is wrong with you, bruh?"

Remington continued to stare at Fallon as he

spoke. "Ain't shit wrong with me, nigga. Why you such a lil' bitch all the time, huh? Everything is always all about you, nigga. Why? You ain't capable of seeing the bigger picture or something?"

Kendrick tried pushing Fallon out of the way so he could get to Remington, but she prepared for that, and she stayed planted in place. Once again, she fought the urge to use her gift and hand out a dose of chill to the two men. Remington continued to stare at Fallon. As angry as he was at her at the moment, she was his peace, and at that moment, he needed all the peace he could get. He clenched his jaw once more before speaking again. "Touch her again and see what happens."

"Nigga, fuck you! You ain't about shit, and in case both y'all forgot, Fallon used to love when I touched her," Kendrick taunted.

Fallon could feel both their emotions, and it was taking everything in her not to fall to her knees from the onslaught of feelings that had been building for centuries. She stood strong and gazed at Remington, whose face tightened at Kendrick's words. "Careful, nigga."

"Fuck you, bruh... for real. The moment I find a slice of happiness, you take that shit from me, man," Kendrick bellowed with tears in his eyes. He was never one to show emotion. He only started doing so when he met Fallon, and he damn sure never did it in front of another nigga, not even Axel, but the shit he was feeling at the moment was too heavy for him. He hated the feeling, and it only made him angry as he watched the love of his life and his brother stare at each other. The shit was breaking him, and he felt like he couldn't breathe. Fallon could feel all that shit, and tears sprang to her eyes as she tried to breathe through it. She wanted to comfort him and calm him down, but she knew he needed to feel this, so she did the only thing she could do… she suffered with him through it.

Remington finally tore his gaze away from Fallon only to meet the anguish in his brother's eyes. Remington shoved some of his anger away before he spoke. "You've only had a couple of weeks to think about this shit, Kendrick. I've had over nine hundred years, my nigga. Nine hundred mothafuckin' years. When I found out Fallon was the woman you were going to marry… do you think I wanted to fuck shit up for you again?"

Kendrick looked away from Remington, clenching his jaw. Remington pounded his chest and yelled, "Look at me, nigga!"

When Kendrick looked back at his brother, tears were falling from his eyes, prompting Remington to swipe at a lone tear that fell from his own eye. "I ain't want to do that shit, bruh. You hear me? I don't live to make your life miserable, nigga. That ain't my MO. I can understand why you might feel that way, but if you remember anything about me, then you know that ain't me. Fallon…"

Remington's voice cracked, and Fallon's shoulders quivered as she silently sobbed. She was trying so hard to be as quiet as possible while she dealt with her own pain as well as the two brothers. She felt like she might pass out, so she held onto Remington's forearm for support while she listened. Remington gave no inclination that he even noticed as he continued. "Fallon is my reason, man. And I know that's hard for you to hear. Believe it or not, it's hard for me to admit that shit to you. Out of all the niggas in the world, Fallon had to go fuck around with my brother. Do you know how that shit hurt *me*? Have you ever thought about how this has all affected *me*?"

Fallon cringed, but she remained quiet. Guilt could consume her later. Right now, she needed to see them through this conversation. She took a deep breath as Remington continued. "If I could have let her go and let y'all be happy, I would have, Kendrick. Believe that shit or not… but I did contemplate it. As much as I hated you for siding with our bitch ass parents all those years ago, I still love you, man… but I couldn't let you bite her, bro. Nine hundred years is a long ass time. It's a long time to contemplate and think about shit… especially when you're completely alone. When I learned Fallon was alive… I started to come get her right then, but I waited it out. I followed y'all a few times, and I peeped how happy you two were. I didn't want to ruin that shit, but when I found out our parents wanted you to turn her, I had to step in."

"Why?" Kendrick shouted. "Why, nigga? Why? You took everything from me!"

Wounded… that was how Kendrick sounded, and it shattered Fallon. He had been holding so much in, and that was the point of this conversation… to finally let it out, for the both of them.

Remington shook his head sadly before he whispered, "Nine hundred years, nigga. Nine hundred years, and one single person was my only reason for surviving. Fuck the fact that I can't die… Fallon is my reason, nigga. I mean that whole heartedly. So much so, that I was willing to allow her to live her life ignorantly and blissfully happy with you, even though I knew that meant an eternity alone for myself."

"She would have been re-born," Kendrick scoffed. "Don't be dramatic."

Realization hit Fallon like a ton of bricks, and she and Remington spoke at the same time.

"No, I wouldn't have."

"No, she wouldn't have."

Kendrick looked at them before asking, "The fuck you mean?"

Fallon gazed up at Remington with fresh tears in her eyes while he stared his brother down. He wasn't as angry anymore… now, he just looked wounded. He stayed quiet, so she turned around and looked at Kendrick. "I wouldn't have been re-born because I didn't have my powers. I technically wasn't a witch… so this would have been my final lifetime."

Kendrick stared down at her. "But—"

"I was willing to let her die without remembering me or where she came from," Remington cut his brother off. "What I wasn't willing to do was allow you to bite her and her to die at your hands. I know what that shit is like, Kendrick. I didn't want that shit for you."

The three of them let the weight of that sink in. There was so much love within this room. Fallon could feel it. It reached out to every corner and crevice, but she could also feel the pain. It was suffocating, and she closed her eyes tightly to try to reign it in while Kendrick whispered, "How do you know she wouldn't have turned if I bit her?"

Remington shook his head sadly. "I think you need to ask yourself why you refused to turn her for four years, bruh. I'm not trying to be an ass when I say this, but that couldn't have been me with the woman I love. I know you wanted an eternity with her, so what was stopping you?"

"I didn't want to be like you, nigga! I didn't want to kill someone I loved," Kendrick snapped.

Again, the three of them let that outburst settle between them before Remington shook his head and said, "This ain't about me, Kendrick. And even if it was about me, let's say the shoe was on the other foot. I'll be honest… if you killed Audrey, that still wouldn't have stopped me from turning Fallon. Let me take it a step further… If I had known how mating bonds worked back then… I would have still bit all y'all, Audrey included."

"You mothafucka," Kendrick said, lunging for Remington, but Fallon shoved him away.

"Stop, Kendrick. I can feel your emotions. They're out of control—"

"Did you hear what he just said? He has no remorse!"

Fallon shook his head. "That isn't what he said, Kendrick. Listen to what he's saying. Put your anger to the side for a moment and just listen."

"If you think for one second I don't regret what happened to Audrey, then you're out of yo' fuckin' mind, Kendrick. I loved my baby sister, and you know that. What I'm saying is when I love someone,

I believe in that love whole heartedly. There's nothing that would stop me from thinking that bond was for an eternity. So, I'll ask again… and be for real… why didn't you bite Fallon?"

Kendrick swiped a hand down his face angrily before he let his head fall back while he looked at the ceiling. "I wasn't sure she would turn. I didn't want to take that risk."

"Right," Remington concluded, and everyone got lost in their own thoughts for a moment before Kendrick spoke again, this time looking at Fallon.

"I didn't want to kill you."

His voice cracked, and he looked so pained that Fallon rushed to him, wrapping him up in a hug. She comforted him the best she could as he cried into her neck. Remington fell back and let them have their moment. When Kendrick settled down some, Fallon pulled away with tears staining her face and said, "Kendrick… it's okay. I forgive you… I just hope one day you can forgive me. I never meant for any of this to happen." Kendrick looked away, but she pulled his gaze back to her, forcing his chin in her direction. "I love you, Kendrick. I do. It's shifted because of the circumstances, but you are still my best friend… don't tell Scarlette that."

He cracked a sad, crooked smile, and Fallon's heart swelled. She loved that smile so much, and in that smile gave her a glimmer of hope for healing in the future. Kendrick pulled away from her and looked at his brother. "You're right. Nine hundred years is a long time. I'm not really sure shit between us can be fixed… but I appreciate you, man. You saved me from myself and made a hard decision for all of us. I respect it."

Kendrick held his hand out to Remington, and Remington cleared his throat trying to get rid of his own emotions, but Fallon could feel them. Remington was beyond relieved. He'd waited a long time to hear words like this from Kendrick, and Fallon was so proud of the both of them.

Remington placed his hand inside Kendrick's, and they shook. Before Fallon could gather what happened, the two were hugging and patting each other on the back as they let more tears fall, doing that manly rocking back and forth shit niggas did when they were emotional and hugging. Fallon sniffled. Her heart was so heavy, and suddenly, she was exhausted. She silently excused herself and allowed the brothers to have their moment. She was going to lay down in bed and try gathering herself before they went to New York.

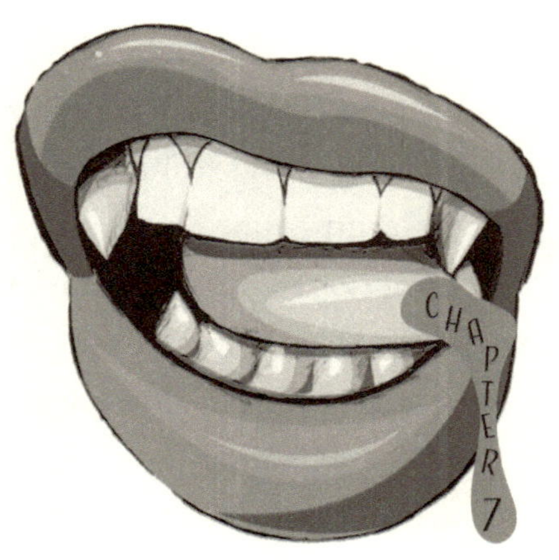

"Y'ALL really don't have to come with," Fallon stressed for what seemed like the thousandth time.

It was now mid-morning, and every vampire that lived in the house was gathered in the kitchen. After the emotional midnight rendezvous in the living room, Fallon had fallen back into a deep sleep. It was odd for a vampire to sleep back to back like that, but with Fallon's gift, she was learning it could leave her with very low energy in times of high emotions. Luckily, she woke up feeling new, and Kendrick and Remington seemed to feel a little lighter, too. Don't get it twisted… they weren't cracking jokes and playing 2K together and shit, but Fallon could sense that the tension was lighter between them, which made her happier than she could even try to explain.

"Please… a trip to New York without needing to take a plane? Sign me up," Scarlette replied.

Fallon rolled her eyes. She really didn't want this to be a huge spectacle. She knew Remington would come with her, but she didn't think every member of The Fang Gang would want to come long, but of course, it was a domino effect. Once Scarlette said she was coming, Axel was on board. Once Axel was on board, so was Kendrick. Papa didn't want to be left out, so his happy ass was tagging along, too, and of course, Calvin would be anywhere Papa was. All Fallon could do was sigh and say, "I don't know what I'm looking for, and where we are going isn't exactly Times Square, Scar. From what I can tell, the location is pretty isolated."

Scarlette shrugged. "I still want to come."

"Alright..." Fallon replied. "Let's get this over with."

Everyone gathered around her. Remington took one of her hands while Scarlette took the other. Everyone else either touched her shoulder or her arm, and before anyone could blink, the rushing feeling of teleporting overtook them before they landed on a dirt road. Immediately, nostalgia overtook Fallon as she looked around while everyone else took their hands off her and took a step back.

"It looks completely different," Remington murmured, and Fallon had to agree. It did look completely different.

"But it feels the same," Fallon replied. She could feel magic humming within the vicinity. It was strong, and Fallon knew that was because her coven made this place home for many lifetimes, leaving behind traces of magic.

"I haven't been here since…" Kendrick let his voice trail off, and Fallon looked at him with sad eyes before walking over and squeezing his shoulder reassuringly.

She was happy when he didn't pull away. Instead, he placed a hand on top of hers and whispered, "Thanks, Beauty."

Tears brimmed Fallon's eyes. It felt like so long since he called her that, and she relished in it. Oddly, she felt it would be the last time. It was an ode to their old life and what could have been. She fully understood that after everything was said and done, she and Kendrick would go their separate ways, and she may not hear him ever say her name again, let alone call her by the nickname he had given her over four years ago when they first met. She pushed back her tears and offered Kendrick a sad smile. He nodded at her with a sad smile of his own before he dropped his arm.

Fallon cleared her throat and looked at Remington, who was looking around, soaking in his surroundings. It hit her how much this trip must have meant to the two Danger brothers. She was sure neither of them had been back since they turned and left the area. This was literally where their origin story began. They were born here, raised here, and all their memories of their baby sister were here. Fallon watched as Remington's eyes landed on a spot several feet ahead of them. He froze, and she walked over to him, gently grabbing his arm. "What is it?"

Before he could respond, Kendrick spoke, and Fallon turned to see him staring at the same spot. "It's where our home used to be."

Scarlette's brows drew together. "How do you know?"

Both brother's shrugged, and everyone noticed how their stances and dispositions were so similar. Remington replied, "Some things you just never forget."

"It just a field of grass," Papa remarked as he kicked a patch of dirt at his feet and looked around.

"Its the way the sun overlooks the field," Kendrick tried to further explain as he walked further into the field. "There used to be other dwellings to the north and south of us. We shared the crops over there," he pointed to the left, "and that's where the animals were."

Remington walked up beside his brother. "We

spent days building the fence for the animals, remember? I had to be no older than eight."

Kendrick snorted. "The blisters and shit I got from chopping all that wood… Father really had us fucked up."

"Ain't that the truth," Remington reminisced with a smile. "And somehow, Audrey never had to do shit. The most she did was help Mama cook."

"Spoiled ass," Kendrick mumbled with a sad smile.

Fallon found it amusing that they started slipping back into the way they used to talk and regard their parents, but she understood. She had never been to this part of the town, but it still felt familiar to her.

The Danger brothers stood for a moment longer before Remington clapped Kendrick on the shoulder, and after a second of hesitation, he pulled Kendrick into his chest by his head. "I love you, kid."

He didn't give Kendrick a chance to respond before he kissed Kendrick on the top of his head and released him before turning around. Kendrick stayed with his back facing the gang, and Fallon saw that he was was discreetly wiping tears away. She let him have his moment and focused on her mate.

"What's the plan, love?" Remington asked.

Fallon hunched her shoulders. "I don't know. I think I need to go by where Lily and I used to live.

The nagging feeling is stronger now that we are here. I just have to figure out what it's trying to tell me."

"Lead the way," Axel said, ready to get this shit over with so they could get to the more important issue at hand… Prima and Maximus.

Fallon felt her phone vibrating in her pants pocket, but she ignored it as she said, "It has to be at least a mile walk from here."

"Nah… more than that I think, love. The farm house was a mile from here, so your dwelling must have been further," Remington corrected.

"Okay, just teleport us there," Scarlette input, grabbing Fallon's hand.

Fallon shook her head and released Scarlette's hand. "I want to walk."

Scarlette and Papa groaned, and Fallon glared at them. "Y'all happy asses wanted to come so bad. Come on."

Begrudgingly, the gang followed while Remington and Fallon lead the way. The walk was peaceful. There were a lot of trees and even more isolated land with crops and fields for days. There were no people, and it was a little too cold for birds and shit. A deer sprinted past them at one point, but other than that, there was no sign of life.

When they walked past where the farm house used to be, Remington and Fallon simultaneously squeezed each other's hands. No words were spoken. They didn't feel they needed to broadcast where their love nest used to be.

Fallon guided them toward her old home, and when they finally made it, she smiled sadly. Like the other areas they came across, it looked completely different, yet... she knew exactly where she was. Some things a person just never forgot, and each home she'd ever had, Fallon would remember. She could picture the small dwelling, and she could see little Lily running around the front yard playing while she cooked dinner. The picture was clear to her, and it made her smile. "This is it."

"Great. A bunch of trees and more dirt," Papa grumbled.

"Hush, Papa," Fallon snapped as she stepped closer to where the dwelling used to be, her gut screaming at her to keep walking forward. As she walked, she reached out and steadied herself on a tree because a rock had gotten stuck on the bottom of her shoe. As soon as her hand connected to the tree, she experienced a vision... something she had yet to experience in this lifetime. She rarely ever got them in past lifetimes, and she forgot how powerful and consuming they could be.

As soon as it was over, her eyes grew wide and focused back on her surroundings. Remington was holding her up and looking at her with worry filled eyes while the rest of the gang gathered around with concern. She peered up at them and said, "Holy shit," before straightening up. "I know exactly why we're here."

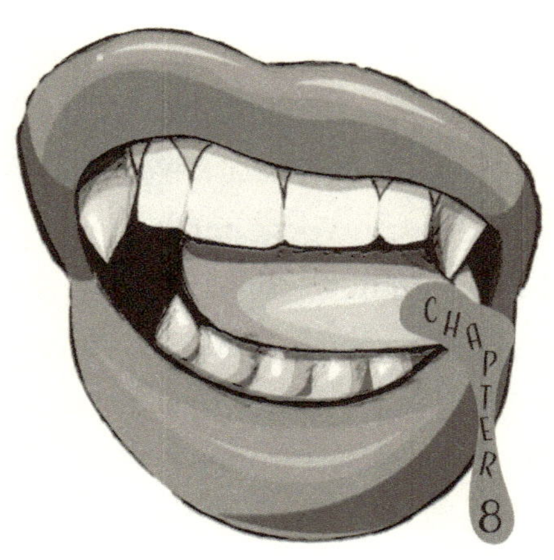

"DON'T JUST STAND THERE, bitch. Tell us. What the fuck just happened?" Papa demanded.

Fallon felt her phone vibrating in her pocket again, but she ignored it and focused on gathering her thoughts. "I had a vision."

Remington's brows knitted together. "I didn't know you could do that."

Fallon shook her head. "Its rare for me. I'm not a seer, so I only see things when extremely necessary. The powers that be must have deemed this necessary... but its odd... this vision was from the past, not the future. Its like it was suppressed or something."

Fallon shook her head again, trying to figure out what other memories were suppressed, if any. She also wondered why she couldn't remember about this tree until now. She understood the need to be punished, but it was like the powers that be were now trying to help her. One thing she knew was she was thankful because this truly was the answer to all their prayers. The powers that be were angry with her, but she also knew they didn't want harm to come to her. Them revealing this memory was proof of that. They just wanted her to learn her lesson, and she had. She promised there would be no more potions or spells to disrupt the natural order of things again. Not by her or anyone she knew. Not on her watch. She wouldn't disappoint them or her coven again.

"Are you just going to stand there? Or are you going to tell us what's up, Fal?" Axel asked.

Fallon cleared her throat and looked at everyone before telling them about her vision.

Over nine hundred years ago

"Powers that beest," Fallon murmured. "Anchor this tree to maketh thee everlasting."

She had her hands on the large white oak tree in front of her dwelling. Lily was asleep, and she was set to meet Remington in just under an hour, but before she could meet her beloved, she followed her intuition to place a safe-guard against her potion. She hadn't had much time to test it and figure out exactly what she was getting herself into, and that made her nervous. She knew she was tapping into some magic that would make her ancestors frown upon her, but she would do anything for the love she and Remington had.

Once the tree was anchored properly, she recited a spell over it, placing her palm on the tree and feeding her magic into the wood. "Hanc arborem vampirism solve fasciculos."

She repeated the incantation five times to seal the magic that would reverse vampirism if ever needed. She knew this potion was strong, which meant there was a chance it was contagious somehow... meaning, she and Remington may not be the only ones effected by it. She knew she needed to have a plan in place to counteract what she was about to put in motion... just in case. After the final incantation was finished, she patted the tree, feeling good about what she had just done. "If it be true it cometh to it, I shall die to reverse everything this potion shall maketh."

The tree hummed with magic, and Fallon was proud of her safeguard, even if it meant her untimely death. With that, she took a deep breath and pushed away her nerves so she could meet her true love and start her new life with the vampirism potions tucked inside her frock.

"I don't get it," Scarlette spoke up after Fallon described her unlocked vision.

Fallon looked up at the tree with tears in her eyes, ignoring her phone that was ringing once again. She knew it had to be her coven because they were the only people not with her who had her number. She silently promised she would call them as soon as she got back home before saying, "The wood from this tree is a weapon." She turned sad eyes toward Remington. "Any of the first ten vampires created can be stabbed by this tree. When they are stabbed, the rest of the original vampires turned within the first full moon of the potion being created would turn to human. When I made this contingency plan, I didn't know how vampirism would work... I didn't know it would create thousands and thousands of vampires. I thought it would only be a few here and there... if that. All I knew was the potion was powerful and would likely have a contagion—"

"So, you, Kendrick, or Remington need to get stabbed?" Axel asked. "But the rest of us would remain vampires because we were created after the first full moon of the potion being created, right?"

"Right, but—"

"Thank God because I was going to have to fight a bitch. I am not about to turn human after finally finding my mate," Papa said as he grabbed Calvin's hand.

"Don't worry, baby. Its an eternity for us," Calvin replied, squeezing his mate's hand.

"Will you guys listen? I took the potion, but I was never turned into a vampire from it. My thinking back then was that I would come back here and stab myself if the vampirism shit wasn't working out… but that can't be the case anymore. It has to be—"

"Me," Remington said before breaking a branch off the tree.

Fallon reached out and snatched the pointed branch from him. "You'll die!"

"What?" he asked. "You said we would be turned to humans. Small price to pay in order to kill Prima and Maximus. They'll be turned to human since I bit them right away… then we can easily kill them—"

"No, Remy," Fallon cut him off. "The person who gets stabbed will die."

Remington stared down at her for a moment before saying, "I can't die."

"And I can't guarantee that'll be true with this magic, Remy. What if this is the loophole? What if this is the one thing that'll kill you?"

Remington cupped her cheek and caressed it softly as he looked at her with sad eyes. "If it'll keep you safe, its a risk I'm willing to take."

Before anyone else could add their two cents, Kendrick flashed over to Fallon and snatched the branch from her, looking at the people he loved most with a hardened expression. "This is how this is going to play out."

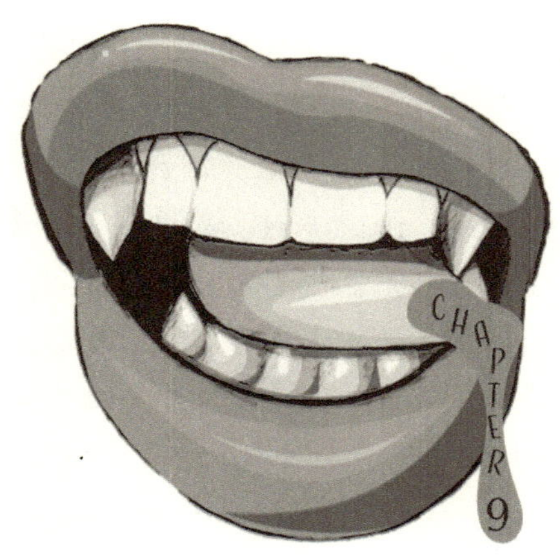

"WHAT YOU DOING, BRO?" Axel asked as he took a tentative step toward Kendrick.

"Yeah... no offense, Kendrick, but you aren't really the most stable nigga to be fucking around with that magical tree branch," Papa interjected before turning to Fallon. "I might have a solution—"

"Papa, man... I love you, bro, but I need you to be quiet for a moment," Kendrick said calmly before turning to everyone else. "I saw—"

"Bro, drop the branch," Remington demanded as he walked up on Kendrick.

"How about everyone stops talking over everyone?" Fallon requested, hugging herself tightly because the emotions whirling around were making her anxious.

"Breathe, love," Remington said over his shoulder, still keeping his eyes on his brother.

Kendrick glanced over Remington's shoulder at Fallon and said, "Breathe, Beauty. This shit ain't going to be easy for you, but you need to breathe."

Fallon's brows furrowed as she wondered what he was talking about, but Remington spoke before she could ask. "Look, man. I don't know what you think is about to happen, but I'm not down with it. Let me get this shit over with so Fallon can teleport us to our shitty ass parents and we can end this shit for good."

Kendrick shook his head and opened his mouth to speak, but Papa slid next to Fallon and started talking to her, so she was only half listening to the argument going on in front of her. "I have something for you."

"Papa, what is it? Now really isn't the time to exchange gifts and shit," Fallon replied as she listened to Remington and Kendrick argue. Her head felt as though it was going to explode, and for the second time that day, she felt exhausted. She didn't know what the fuck to do about the situation unfolding in front of her. One of the Danger brothers would have to die and the other would have to turn into a human in order for them to have a solid chance of killing Prima and Maximus. There had to be another way, and if she could only control the emotions she was feeling and have a moment to think, she was sure she would figure it out, but Papa stood in her line of vision and stole her attention.

"Fallon, listen," he snapped before shoving something into her hand.

She looked down at it, and her eyes widened. "I don't know what is about to happen or which way this is going to go... obviously, Remington is your mate, so you probably won't need this, right? But Kendrick.. we just don't know, right? He could be your mate, but how would we know? This could help, though, right? I don't want either of them to die, Fal—"

"Papa... what... how?" Fallon stumbled over her words.

Papa gave her a crooked grin as they both stared down at the cure Fallon had given him a few weeks ago. He grabbed at the back of his neck before saying, "Yeah... so... turns out that night I turned Calvin... I was so drunk I could have sworn I slipped this into his drink, but I didn't. I found this the next morning in my pants pocket and something told me to keep it on me at all times... I guess I have a bit of that witchy intuition you're always talking about, huh?"

Fallon's wide eyes misted over as she looked at Papa and then to Calvin before gazing back at Papa. "You found your true mate?"

Papa nodded his head before glancing back at Calvin. "I did… I was just as surprised as you are."

Fallon was blown away. She and the entire gang had thought he turned Calvin with the help of the cure she created. They were all wrong, and she was in awe. "Why didn't you say anything?"

He shrugged. "It didn't seem important. I got my mate… that was all that mattered to me."

Fallon reached up and hugged him around his neck. "I'm so happy for you, Papa." When she pulled away, she wiped a tear and said, "Yes, this should help… but I can't risk one of them dying. I just need a moment to think—"

Fallon's phone rang again as Kendrick and Remington's voices got louder.

"I won't let you do this shit, man! You're my lil' bro… drop the branch, nigga!" Remington shouted.

"I told you I already saw how this shit is going to play out. Step the fuck back, bro," Kendrick snarled.

"You can't see me, though, nigga! You can't see me or Fallon, so whatever you saw may not be full proof—"

"Trust me, dawg. This is. You just have to trust me on this, bro. Remember what we talked about this morning. I forgive you, aight?" Kendrick said sadly, but he was standing his ground and not backing down.

"Man, fuck that!" Remington snapped.

The two were close to blows, and Fallon wanted to step in, but the insistent ringing of her phone was driving her insane matched with the high emotions, so she snatched it out of her pocket and answered it without comprehending who was even calling. "What?"

"Fallon!" a voice cried.

Fallon pulled the phone away from her ear and looked down at it. She saw it was Samiyah calling before she placed it back to her ear. "I'm a little busy, Samiyah. What—"

"We located Prima and Maximus earlier," Samiyah interrupted. They were in New Orleans hiding out, but about an hour ago they were suddenly in New York... like they were teleported there. You said you were going to New York today, so we were worried, and we lost track of them like they fell off the face of the Earth just after they teleported. It's like they're using magic or something—"

"Where in New York?" Fallon asked as panic settled in her chest.

It sounded like The Guild had more witches at their disposal, and that was dangerous because it meant they could track the gang and get around quickly by teleportation. She scanned the area as her nerves were on high alert. Her eyes landed on a place several feet away where the air seemed to glimmer slightly. She could sense magic there, and she gasped just as Samiyah said, "Hamilton County, which was why we were worried. It's right where we used to reside, and we knew you were going there. Do you need us to come—"

Fallon was barely listening to Samiyah. Her eyes stayed trained on the spot several spots away that hummed with magic. "Stay where you're at. I'll call you back."

Fallon disconnected the call before Samiya could respond. She didn't want to put her coven sisters in harms way once again because she saw this situation for what it was… an ambush.

"Revelare," she murmured at the same time the tree behind her went up in flames and The Guild was revealed, ready to attack.

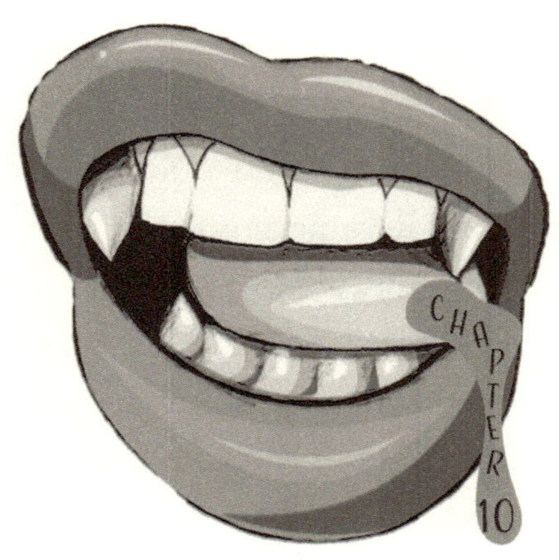

"LOOKS like the little witch finally caught on, dear," Prima spoke as she took a step forward.

"Unfortunately for her, it was too late," Maximus replied. "We heard everything, and now your precious tree will die with you."

Fallon quickly stuffed the cure into her pocket before running over to Kendrick, all while keeping an eye on the ops. They had a warlock with them this time. He didn't seem to be afraid like the last witch they got to do their bidding, but he didn't seem like he wanted to be there. Aside from him, there were nine other vampires, not including the king and queen.

"Stab one of them with it," Fallon murmured low enough for only Kendrick to hear.

The idea should have come to her much sooner. It was a no brainer. The best shot they had at this was to kill Maxima or Prima with the branch Kendrick had in his hand. Then, the remaining parent, Kendrick, and Remington would become human. Fallon would bite Remington on the strength that he is her mate, and she could give Kendrick the cure and bite him. It was the best shot they had, but Fallon became confused when he slightly shook his head. Their moment passed, though, because within a millisecond, The Guild was on them, and a fight broke out between them and the gang.

Fallon caught a glimpse of Kendrick, who dropped the branch on the ground just as his father connected his fist to his jaw. Fallon didn't have time to help him because Prima was running toward her full speed. Fallon simply stepped to the side, and Prima ran right past her and tackled the ground before gracefully bouncing right back up with an evil grin on her face. "You realize you'll never kill us, right?"

Fallon didn't speak, she simply sent out a wave of anxiety, doing her best to target Prima only. She dropped to her knees and grasped at her chest. "What... are you... doing to me?"

Out of the corner of her eye, Fallon saw Scarlette fall to her knees along with two male vampires that were fighting her. She tried to reel the emotion in and only aim it toward the enemies, but as she tried focusing on that, another vampire sideswiped her head, causing her the emotions to snap back into her. She flew several feet before she landed on her toes lightly, facing Prima again, who was now standing and rubbing at her chest. Fallon ran toward her while she was still distracted and punched her square in the nose. She flew back into a nearby tree, completely breaking it in half and landing on her back, but she quickly got back up again. "You little bi—"

Something tugged at Fallon's heart, causing her head to whip toward Remington. It was crazy how amidst all the chaos and emotions, Remington could be felt above all that shit. Maximus and another vampire had Remington in a bind. The unknown male vampire held him down while Maximus was tugging at his head, trying to pull it off while Kendrick stood off to the side looking frozen in place. She knew instantly that Maximus had him under his control, which wasn't a good thing because he was the one with the weapon. She glanced at the burning tree and whispered, "Exstinguere."

The tree instantly stopped burning, but she wasn't sure there was any oak left to salvage. She glanced back at Remington with worry. Fallon knew he couldn't die, but that didn't mean it wasn't her automatic reaction to come to his aid. Unfortunately for her, just that fast she forgot about Prima, who took advantage of her being distracted. The queen grabbed Fallon by the throat and squeezed tightly. "Why doesn't my touch effect you?"

Fallon glared at her before channeling her magic into her hand and placing it on Prima's forearm. Instantly, the queen's arm went up in flames, and she released her hold on Fallon. Fallon straightened up and stared down at Prima, who was rolling around on the ground trying to extinguish the fire. "Because I made you, bitch."

Fallon was about to light the rest of Prima's body on fire, but another tug at her heart directed her attention to her mate. He was still struggling, so Fallon left Prima on the ground and dodged Papa and Calvin who were tag teaming a guild member before she reached Remington. She punched the nigga who was holding her man down straight in the side of the head, which caused him to let go. Remington repositioned himself and body slammed his father, cracking the earth with the force while Fallon grabbed the other vampire by the head while he was still on the ground. She twisted, and his head effortlessly detached from his body. Remington and Maximus were going at it, and Remington seemed to be holding his own, so Fallon rushed over to Kendrick so she could try to snap him out of his compulsion.

"Kendrick!" She waved her hand in front of his face, but he stood still, not even blinking. She blew out a breath of frustration before putting her hand in his hoodie pocket for the branch… but it was gone. "No… no, no, no…"

Panic filled her as she took a quick glance around. Several of The Guild members were dead, including the unknown warlock they had with them. The gang was still intact, but they were barely hanging on. Scarlette was now dodging Prima, who was trying to use her gift on her. Papa and Calvin looked to be losing a fight with two guild members. Axel was fighting a bitch who seemed to have more combat skills than him. The only one who looked like they were doing okay was Remington. He was beating his father's ass into the damn ground. Had the situation not been dire, Fallon would have been so proud of her man, but she couldn't focus on that at the moment. She turned back to Kendrick and harshly whispered, "Kendrick! What happened to the branch? Where is it?"

He stared ahead blankly, and Fallon got frustrated. She reached out and grabbed his arm. "Kendrick!"

As soon as she touched him, he shook his head and blinked several times before looking at her. "Fallon?"

Fallon looked down at her hand on his arm and realized she had rid him of the compulsion with just a simple touch. Remington had been sure her blocking was different from his, and he was right. She was able to reverse the gifts of the other original vampires. She wasn't sure how exactly it worked, and she didn't have time to dissect it now. She placed her hand on Kendrick's cheek and whispered, "Kendrick, where is the branch? We have to stab one of them before they kill one of us—"

Kendrick's eyes seemed to focus and then harden when she mentioned the branch. He grabbed her hand and placed a kiss on her palm. "I saw every version of how this would play out, Fallon. Trust me when I say this is the only way."

Before Fallon could process what he was doing, he pulled the branch out from the sleeve of his hoodie and plunged the pointed half into his stomach.

"No!" The scream that tore from Fallon's being was filled with so much agony and pain, a powerful blast emanated from her and forced everyone and everything within a hundred foot radius to fly back as she caught Kendrick and gently laid him on the ground. Once she knew he was as comfortable as he could be, she stood up with a hardened expression. It was time to end this shit.

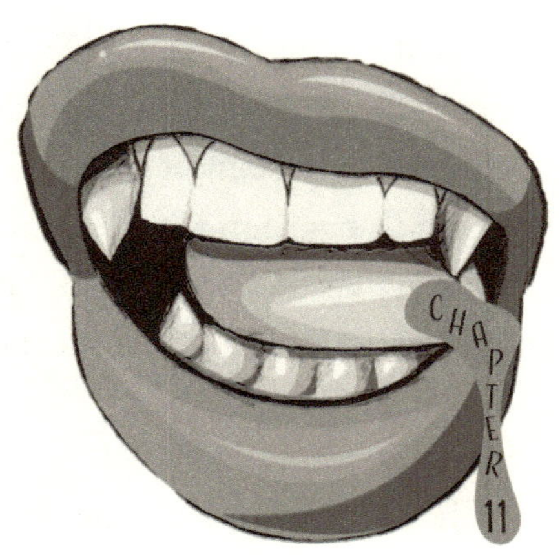

AXEL AND SCARLETTE were easily able to get up after the blast from Fallon. They looked at each other before Axel asked, "You good, sis?"

"Yeah," Scarlette breathed. "What the fuck just happened?"

Axel looked around and saw Fallon stomping toward Prima, who was lying on the ground. "My guess is Fallon had another one of her fits."

Neither of them had time to fully process what was going on before their focus shifted to the final three vampires stalking toward them, while Papa and Calvin ran to intercept them. They geared up for another fight while Fallon wiped her tears from across the field and made her final step toward Prima. Her heart tugged at her to look toward Remington, but she couldn't make herself do so. She

91

could feel he was still alive, even though the connection was weak. Still, that was enough to give her entire focus to the bitch in front of her.

Prima was on the ground with a tree branch piercing her midsection and blood leaking from her forehead. Fallon stared down at her as she coughed up blood.

"Wha… what did you… do?"

Fallon crouched down and put her hand on the part of the tree that was piercing Prima before she pushed it further into her. Prima let out an ear-piercing cry, and Fallon stared at her while she withered in agony. Fallon had never been one for blood and gore… but at that moment, she was a certified psychopath. Blood didn't faze her. It actually excited her, which was why she kept pushing the branch into Prima until it was embedded in the ground below her.

Prima's breaths came out in harsh puffs as she peered up at Fallon. As a last ditch effort, she reached out and grabbed Fallon's forearm, and Fallon laughed. "You haven't gotten the hint yet? You're human, Prima. Your time is up."

"The… tree," she gasped, and Fallon chuckled.

"Y'all must not have been paying close enough attention when you were spying on us. Fuckin' idiots. We had a branch before your warlock friend burned the tree. Your son… sacrificed himself—" Fallon's voice cracked, and she shook the emotion away. "It doesn't matter. Any last words?"

Prima's gaze hardened as she attempted to pull the wooden branch out of her. Fallon had to admit, her will to live was astronomical. When she realized that wouldn't work, she moved her tear-filled eyes to Fallon and said, "Fuck y—"

Fallon didn't allow her to finish. She snapped her neck quickly with the flick of her wrist before she dashed over to Maximus, who had just made it to his feet. Fallon slammed him back down to the ground by palming his forehead. She took care not to put all her force into it so he wouldn't die on impact. He groaned and then struggled to get up, but Fallon was much stronger than him now.

"Bitch ass nigga," Fallon spat.

"What did you do to me? Why does it hurt so much?" he asked in a panic.

Fallon chuckled before kicking him in his ribs. She felt the bones cracking under the force of her kick, and a moment later, he was coughing up blood like his wife had only moments ago. "You forgot what its like to be human?"

"Hu.. man?" he sputtered. "H-how?"

A lump formed in her throat when she thought about Kendrick. It had only been a minute since he drove the branch into his abdomen, and she left him alive. She realized she didn't have time to draw out Maximus' torture. She needed to get to Kendrick and check on Remington. Frustrated with the thought of Maximus having a quick death, Fallon bared her teeth and snarled, "Say hi to your wife in hell for me."

A look of horror crossed his features as he frantically looked around the field as best he could, searching for Prima, but that was short lived because Fallon placed her foot at his neck before she applied pressure, crushing all the bones there and then completely decapitating him.

As soon as Maximus took his last breath, the three vampires that were fighting Scarlette, Axel, and Papa stopped. The gang took that opportunity to fuck them up, but Fallon heard the other vampires screaming, "We surrender! We surrender!"

That right there let Fallon know that none of the members of The Guild were working for the king and queen on their own free will. The compulsion died with Maximus, but Fallon wasn't worried about that. She ran over to Kendrick and dropped to her knees just as Axel and Scarlette joined her side while Calvin and Papa made sure the three vampires stayed on the ground.

"What the fuck happened?" Axel snarled as he tried pushing Fallon out of the way, but Scarlette stopped him and held him back as she watched on with tears in her eyes.

Fallon ignored them and grabbed Kendrick's hand while tears fell from her eyes. He was still alive but barely.

"Kenny, look at me," she murmured as she grabbed his chin and forced his gaze to her.

He smiled softly as his eyes focused on her. "Beauty…"

"Shh…" Fallon said before choking on a sob. "Don't talk, Kenny. They're dead. I killed them. I love you."

He looked like he wanted to respond, but he wasn't able to as blood pooled in the corners of his mouth. Fallon quickly moved out of the way and looked at Axel. "Bite him."

"Wha—"

"He was able to turn you. Turn him, Axel. Do it now before he dies!" Fallon cried before she reached into her pocket and pulled out the cure. "Give this to him first."

Axel wasted no time crouching next to Kendrick and opening his mouth before pouring the potion in.

Kendrick coughed it right back up, and a sob escaped Fallon. She knew the cure was a long shot, anyway, but it was the best shot they had to save him.

"Shit," Axel exclaimed.

"Bite him anyway, Axel. He's dying," Scarlette said with a cry, and Axel wasted no time biting Kendrick's neck, draining his blood. Fallon sat back on her ass and rocked back and forth while she watched. Tears poured from her face because she knew what Axel was doing was of no use. She had created the magic within the oak… it was a spell to reverse vampirism. Any vampire with the magic from the oak flowing through them wouldn't adhere to vampire venom, but she had to try something. Her heart ached tremendously as she watched Axel back away from his best friend with tears in his eyes while Scarlette held onto him.

Each of them could see Kendrick wasn't breathing. They all knew Axel's bite didn't work, but none of them were ready to accept it. Another tug at Fallon's heart caused her to stand up and stumble backward.

"I'm sorry," she mumbled as she back pedaled before she completely turned on her heels and ran toward Remington. Once again, she dropped to her knees and let out a cry. "Baby," she whispered.

Remington looked weak. She could tell the blast

immediately after turning human really fucked him up. She lifted his head gingerly and saw blood there. She stifled another cry before saying, "Just hold on, love. I got you."

He didn't respond. He simply closed his eyes, now at peace that he was in the arms of the woman he loved. His safe place.

Fallon bit his neck and sucked. His human blood revived her. She could feel energy and strength filling her with each sip she took. Remington didn't put up a fight as she drained him, and when she was finished, she pulled away slightly and cried tears of relief at the rise and fall of his chest. He was still alive. She had been nervous because she wasn't sure the rules about a person turning twice. She knew the powers that be were angry about the entire thing, but she also felt she had been punished enough. Maybe they felt that way too and allowed her this win.

She stood to her feet and lifted Remington into her arms bridal style. If she wasn't in so much pain over losing Kendrick, she might laugh at the shit. If Remington could see himself right now, he would be pissed, but nothing about this moment was funny.

She dashed over to Scarlette and Axel. "Grab onto me and Kendrick. Papa, Calvin, come on."

Axel did as he was told while Scarlette grabbed onto Fallon's shoulder. Papa and Calvin were at her side and holding onto her within a second. The last thing Fallon saw before she teleported back to The Lair were the three surviving vampires kneeling several yards away from her. They looked up just in time for her to disappear and saluted who they considered to be their new queen.

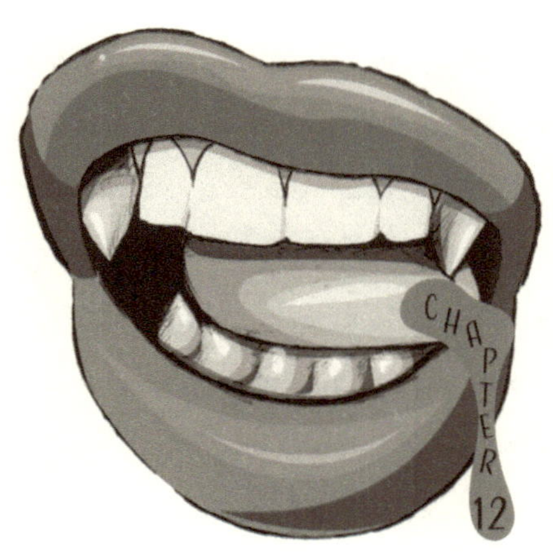

Beauty,

I'm writing this just after Remington and I had our heart to heart. While I was hugging him... healing with him, and finally getting a little hope for the future... it was all snatched away from me with the foresight of what was to come. What I saw was blotchy, and I can only imagine that's because you and Remington are somehow involved. For the first time, I was shown different outcomes and variations for what would happen when we went to New York. If I alerted you that The Guild was following us, the outcome would have lead to you dying. I couldn't see it exactly, because my gift does not work on you, but I saw a future without you in it, and that was confirmation enough for me. If I ventured off and tried fighting them off alone, Maximus would have used his power on me, and Remington would have ended up in captivity for eternity. I'm not sure why I was suddenly able to see him... maybe it is because our connection was restored? If Remington would have stabbed himself with the oak, both Axel and Scarlette would have died... it had to be me, Beauty. I know you are struggling to understand why, and I wish I was here to help you understand, baby... but this is it for me, and honestly, I'm okay with that because I don't know what a life without you by my side looks like. I was given the gift of foresight, but since you've been snatched away from me, I haven't been able to see a thing... not even my future.

Before, when we were together and happy... I saw a future with you. It may not have been an eternity, but it was a comfortable future where I watched you age and gave you a life full of love and happiness. I was content with that because I knew without a doubt you were my one greatest love. I still believe that, which is why I am at peace with the sacrifice I have to make. This is the only scenario that allows you and my brother to live in love and peace. You deserve that. I'm only sorry I wasn't man enough to create that life for you.

Just know I love you. I always have, and even in the past weeks where I've been distant, it's only because my love for you burns so bright. Don't cry over me, Fallon. Smile when you think of me and remember the good times. Remember the laughs... you were the only person to ever make me laugh. Remember the long nights of terrible vampire movies and shows that I secretly loved. Remember the nights where we would get fucked up and be on some gang gang shit with the crew. Man... I love y'all.

Even though I'm gone... I love y'all. That will never change. On some real corny shit... I ain't ever gonna leave y'all because I'm a part of y'all. Gang for life, you hear me?

Be good to yourself and thrive, baby. For me.

P.S. Take care of my brother. He's a tough ass nigga, but he's soft in a lot of ways. Tell him I said I love him. I always have and always will. I'll give Audrey a hug and kiss for him.

P.S.S. Keep an eye on Axel for me, too. I know he's going to hurt over this one. It might be time for him to settle down and find a mate. Help him see that, Fal.

P.S.S.S. Take that mothafuckin' throne, queen. Change the world and shit. You're destined, Beauty. I always knew it. Don't be afraid, and get that shit done!

Love for an eternity,

Kendrick - Gang Gang!

FALLON WIPED a lone tear that fell from her eye as she closed the folded letter from Kendrick for the hundredth time. Every day had been a fight to stay positive and try to find the silver lining in everything that happened, and every day depression seemed to be winning more and more. Two weeks had passed, and just like she had made no progress on accepting the fact that Kendrick was gone, Remington had made no progress on waking up. He was still breathing, but he had yet to open his eyes, and Fallon was losing hope as each day went on. All kinds of scenarios filled her mind as she wondered why things had to play out like this. Whenever she got too caught up in the why of how everything unfolded, she read the letter Kendrick left for her, hoping it would bring new answers. It never did. She had yet to accept the fact that Kendrick really did make the ultimate sacrifice for not only her, but the entire gang, and that only made her feel guilty because if only Kendrick had been happy… maybe he would have fought harder to stay alive.

She sighed heavily and held back the onslaught of tears threatening to spill over as she glanced down at Remington, who appeared to be sleeping peacefully in their bed. Fallon knew better, though. She knew how painful turning was, and Remington's body had been at it for two weeks. She leaned down and caressed his face. "It's going to be okay, my love."

Although she spoke the words, she wasn't sure she believed them. She wasn't sure anything would be alright ever again. She glanced down at the letter in her hand once again before she reached over and tucked it in the nightstand drawer.

Axel had been after her the past several days about laying Kendrick to rest, but Fallon had been adamant that they needed to wait until Remington woke up. They were brothers, and she knew Remington would want to be there to say a final goodbye. Axel had been understanding for the most part, but he was struggling with the loss of his best friend, too, and she knew he needed the closure.

Fallon glanced down at Remington and whispered, "Please wake up, baby."

She laid down and cuddled up to him, rubbing his chest, trying to offer him some comfort, before exhaustion overtook her, and she fell into a deep sleep.

Not even an hour had gone by before Fallon woke to a hand caressing her face. Her eyes popped open and met Remington's brown ones. She gasped and sat up straight, nearly knocking him over as she wrapped her arms around his neck. "You're awake!"

He chuckled. "And thirsty as hell. What the fuck happened?"

Fallon clung to him with tears in her eyes. "Remy... oh, my God. I can't believe you're awake!"

"I'm assuming I turned to human?" he asked. "I don't remember shit. I know I was fighting Maximus, but after that everything is blank. How long has it been?"

"Two weeks. I wasn't sure you would ever wake up," Fallon whispered, and Remington pulled her close, kissing her on the head before pulling away and wiping her tears.

"I'm here, baby. I'm sorry you had to worry. I could feel your presence the entire time I was turning. I had forgotten how much that shit hurts." His tongue flicked out to touch his fangs. "And how thirsty I would be. I wonder if I still have my gifts..."

His sentence trailed off as they sat in their own thoughts for a moment before Fallon spoke.

"I'll get you a human—" She had started to get off the bed so she could teleport, but Remington stopped her.

"Wait. Tell me what happened first, baby. Which one of them got the white oak to the heart?" He sounded amused, and Fallon choked back a sob while she shook her head. His smile morphed into a frown. "What? What is it?" Fallon stayed silent as she tried to find her words. She didn't want to be the one to tell him about Kendrick, but she also knew she was the only one who should. Remington could feel her pain and panic, and as if a lightbulb went off in his head, he asked, "Where is Kendrick?" Tears filled Fallon's eyes while Remington grabbed her shoulders and shook her. "Where's my brother, Fallon?"

"He's dead," she finally blurted out, and Remington stilled as he closed his eyes while tears fell down his cheeks.

"I was supposed to protect him," he mumbled. "I was supposed to protect him and my sister… and I failed. I—"

Fallon stopped him. "No, baby… no." She cupped his cheeks and waited patiently until he looked into her eyes. "Kendrick foresaw what was going to happen, Remy. He chose this… for us." Remington looked confused, and Fallon sighed heavily. "He left me a note explaining everything."

Remington shook his head, but she could tell he was coming to terms with what she said. Maybe one day she would share his letter with Remington, but it felt so intimate and personal. For now, she wanted to focus on helping comforting Remington. She wasn't sure the love Kendrick expressed to Fallon would be comforting to his brother.

Remington lifted his watery gaze to Fallon's green eyes and said, "I need to say goodbye."

Fallon's heart broke because she could feel Remington's breaking. She knew the guilt Remington felt would consume him, but she would focus on one thing at a time. Healing wouldn't happen in one day.

"We haven't had a funeral yet. We waited for you," she replied, wiping his tears.

"Thank you," he murmured.

"How about we go feed and then I tell you everything that happened? Axel will be happy you're awake so we can move on with the funeral, but planning that can wait until tomorrow, okay?"

"Okay," he whispered, and Fallon pushed out a small dose of happiness toward him. It wasn't much… just a little nudge. Truthfully, it was all she could muster because she herself was bogged down with emotion.

He smiled at her then grabbed her hand, squeezing it gently before wiping the rest of his tears with his other hand and saying, "Take me to the nearest human."

Fallon offered him a soft smile. "Anything for you, my love."

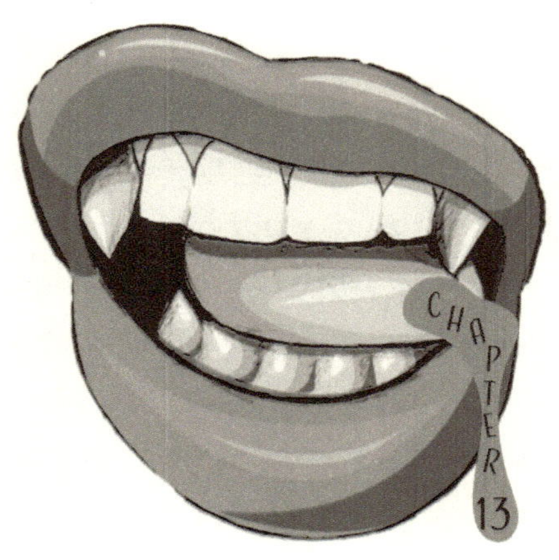

THE HUMIDITY in the air made Fallon's curls frizz out. Her skin was damp with moisture as she looked up at the grey sky. The humidity was a sure sign of rain, and she wished mother nature would get on with it already because the humid heat was not it, especially since she, the gang, and some of her coven had spent the last hour outside saying their goodbyes to Kendrick.

The funeral was intimate, but the people that mattered were there. The mood was somber, but this day was needed in order for healing to begin. It had been two days since Remington woke up, and he and Axel worked together to put together the perfect goodbye…. gang style.

They'd settled on laying Kendrick to rest right there in New Orleans, since it was where the gang decided to remain. They wanted to be able to visit

Kendrick as often as possible. The idea to have him buried back in New York where he was born was also on the table, but they decided against it since it got cold there, so that would make it so the gang couldn't visit him during those cooler months. They did, however, plant an everlasting tree that Fallon embedded with magic to last for an eternity in Kendrick's memory at the location of his childhood home. She was very careful not to do anything more than make the tree everlasting. She knew she was on thin ice, fucking with the natural order of things, and she didn't want anymore beef with the powers that be or karma… that hoe was a whole ass bitch.

NOLA was where the gang resided, so that was where they decided to put Kendrick to rest. It was also where Fallon met Kendrick and where Remington and Kendrick made amends. It was perfect, and the plot they got for him wasn't far from The Lair.

Kendrick's casket was sleek black, and the interior was blood red. He looked so handsome in his black suit, and each member left something with him in his casket. Fallon left her engagement ring he'd gotten her with him. It hurt to leave it behind, but she knew it would bring Kendrick comfort in the afterlife, so she did so with no hesitation. Scarlette and Papa got together and made him a little scrapbook of their times through the years along with a handwritten letter. Axel left the embroidered biker jacket Kendrick got for the entire gang with their names on it, and Remington left a necklace he found that belonged to Audrey in Kendrick's room. He recognized it immediately, because it was one Remington had made for her and gifted to her himself. He cried for hours when he found it, but he knew he couldn't be selfish and hold onto it.

As soon as everyone said their goodbyes, Fallon and a few of her coven sisters magically filled the grave. Samiyah then crouched down and touched her hand to the freshly filled Earth. Instantly, green grass grew along with some Lily flowers. When she finished, she stood and nodded before teleporting.

The rest of the coven did the same, leaving the gang alone. Fallon cleared her throat and looked at everyone with sad eyes. "Ready?"

There were a few nods before they gathered around her, and she teleported them to The Lair, where her coven sisters had gathered. There was food and music, and Fallon knew it was time to really get the celebration of life started. She wished she were more in the partying mood, but she was glad to see that Papa, Calvin, Axel, and Scarlette were at least. Papa and Scarlette were able to drown their sorrows in liquor. Fallon had tried that, and it only made her more emotional, so she opted out of the celebration and excused herself to the coven room after receiving some condolences from her coven sisters.

Once inside the peace of the coven room, Fallon sighed and walked over to the bay window and looked out at the sky as the sun steadily dipped below the horizon. Fresh tears brimmed her eyes as she thought about all she had gained and lost in the past few months. Her head hurt when she sat too long with those kinds of thoughts because it was such a tangled web. Luckily, she didn't have to because she felt Remington's presence behind her, and without even turning around, she asked, "Why aren't you taking shots in memory of Kendrick with the gang?"

His large hands circled around her waist from behind, and he kissed her cheek. "I'll leave that to them. Kendrick and I never had the chance to get fucked up together. No reason to start now."

Fallon chuckled before turning around and circling her arms around his neck. "How are you?"

He shrugged. "Could be better, but one day at a time, right?"

"That's right," Fallon murmured.

They stayed like that for a moment, basking in each other's presence and staring into each other's eyes before Remington said, "I'd much rather focus on the future with you, love."

Fallon cocked her head to the side. "Meaning?"

"Meaning what is our next move? The Guild is dismantled, and the vampires need a leader to maintain order. The coven is looking at you to step into that position to bridge the gap."

Fallon sighed. She had been thinking a lot about that, especially since Kendrick made it his dying wish and all. She looked up at Remington and asked, "You really think I could do that?"

He chuckled. "You can do anything, baby. You really are the most powerful being in the world. Half vampire… half witch. You know… that means if we have kids, they'll be vampire and witch, too."

Fallon thought about it for a moment. "Kids, huh?"

He pulled her closer. "Oh yeah. A gang of them."

Fallon giggled while shaking her head. "One thing at a time, love."

Remington turned to look out the window while still holding on to the love of his life. Just as the sun dipped below the horizon he whispered, "We have an eternity to figure it out."

Fallon snuggled into him and watched the moon take its place as she thought about Kendrick and Lily. It was at that moment she realized why humans believed life was short. She never really listened to it even before she turned. She always lived life carefree and day to day, but now that everything was said and done, she understood. It wasn't the end she had hoped for, but it was what she had been dealt, and now, she had an eternity to live with it.

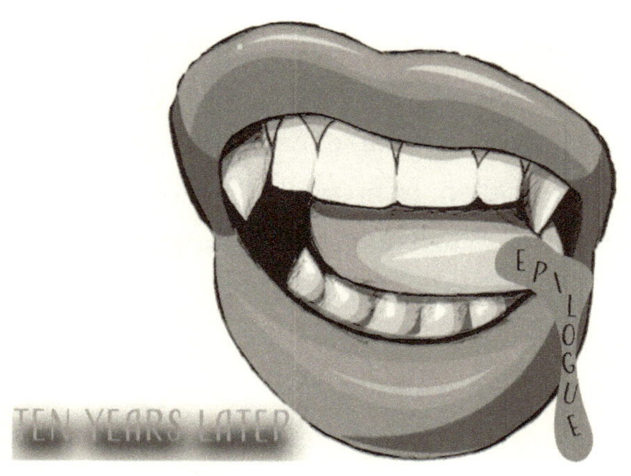

"YOU READY, BABY?" Remington said softly, even though Fallon was upstairs, as their six year old son whizzed passed him. He snapped his hand out and caught him to prevent him from running off and hiding somewhere. "KD, settle down, man. We have to get going."

Kendrick Bordeaux Danger looked up at his father with bright green eyes and freckles strewn across his face before scrunching his little nose and saying, "Ligare."

Instantly, Remington's hands were bound, and Kendrick was running off again.

"That lil' mothafucka," Remington grumbled just as Fallon made her appearance near the front door where he was struggling.

She took one look at her husband before she cursed under her breath and yelled, "KD! Bring your ass here right now! Don't make me use my magic!"

KD, as they called him, walked into the foyer with his head held down, and Fallon tapped her foot impatiently. "What did I tell you about using your magic on us?"

"That it's rude," he mumbled.

"Boy, unbind your father before I beat your lil' behind," Fallon snapped.

KD waved his hand toward his father, and in an instant, his hands were free. Since turning human and becoming a vampire again, Remington had lost his gifts, and spells now worked on him... all of them, which was a pain in the ass because KD surprised them both when he was born a warlock with not an ounce of vampirism in him. As soon as his little ass turned two, his powers came to him, and they were powerful as fuck.

"Apologize to your father," Fallon seethed.

KD walked slowly toward Remington and hugged his midsection. "I'm sorry, Daddy."

Remington crouched down and looked his son in the eye. Aside from the green eyes and freckles, he looked just like Kendrick, the man he was named after, and his heard pained a bit each time he looked at him. "You're forgiven, Son, but we need to learn to

control those powers and only use them when necessary, okay?"

"Okay, Daddy," Kendrick agreed before turning
to face his mother with big sad eyes.

Fallon smacked her lips and rolled her eyes. "Both
of y'all get on my nerves."

Remington straightened up walked over to his
wife before placing his hand on her swollen stomach.
They had been married for eight years and had KD
soon after. Now, she was pregnant again and
miserable.

"What did I do?" Remington asked.

Fallon pointed to her stomach. "You put twins in
me, asshole."

"Ohh, Mama!" KD sang, and Fallon cut her eyes
at him. Everything had been irritating her lately, and
she just knew she wasn't to make it through this
pregnancy without going a little bit insane. She was
six months, but three more months of this sounded
like hell to her.

"Hush, boy," she said to KD before saying, "Y'all
ready?"

Both of them nodded before she grabbed their
hands and teleported them to Texas where Julianne
lived. She was twenty years old now and thriving as
a seer. Back when Fallon was pregnant with KD, they
decided to do a baby reveal ceremony where they

could find out if Fallon was carrying a new witch or someone she already knew. It had been a millennia since she had been able to do one of them, and she was excited to have Julianne do her first ceremony for Fallon. They'd been surprised to learn Fallon was carrying the first warlock of the coven.

This time around, both Fallon and Remington were curious to see not only what gender their babies were but if they would also be witches or warlocks instead of vampires.

They landed right outside Julianne's door. She lived in a quaint town with a modest home. Just before Fallon could knock, the door swung open, and Julianne was pulling her in for a hug.

"Oh my goodness, it's been so long," Julianne said.

Fallon hugged her back and replied, "I know, I'm sorry. Things have been so busy—"

Julianne pulled away and waved her off. "You're the queen of the paranormal… don't apologize."

Fallon blushed, still not used to the title after all these years. It took a lot of time and organizing, but she and Remington officially took the throne as king and queen, not only over the vampires, but over all witches as well. They ruled over anyone who wasn't human, and it was a taxing job. Luckily, she had the gang backing her and helping out in numerous ways.

Scarlette was still single and threw herself into her position as the liaison for the vampires, but Fallon could sense that her bestie was thinking about settling down. When she decided to make that leap, Papa and Calvin had her covered. They oversaw the creation of the cure and distributed it to fitting vampires as they saw fit. There was a whole process involved and protocols in place to ensure a balance that suited the witches, vampires, and humans alike. Axel had surprisingly mated to a beautiful Jamaican woman a few years back, and they oversaw the new paranormal prison that was built. Shit was good, but life was hectic as hell, and Fallon was a bit nervous to go from a mommy of one to three.

Julianne invited them in and then hugged both Remington and KD before crouching down so she was eye-level with KD. "I have a new potion kit that needs to be opened."

KD's eyes lit up before he turned to his parents. "Can I?"

"It's a kid one, right?" Fallon asked wearily. There were many shops that created toys for child warlocks and witches, and she just had to be sure this was one of them. If Julianne gave KD access to an actual potion kit, he was liable to blow the entire house up.

Julianne chuckled. "Of course it is. It's in the coven room with a bow on it."

KD's smile was wide as he raced out of the room while the adults got comfortable in the living room.

"Should we get to it?" Julianne asked.

"Yes, please. I'm anxious," Fallon replied, and Julianne nodded.

"Get comfortable on the couch."

Fallon did as she was told, lying her head in Remington's lap and looking up at him. They smiled at each other. Love between them was so easy. The past decade had been hectic, but they always remembered to love on each other.

He brushed her ginger curls out of her face while Julianne kneeled on the floor next to them, placing her hand on Fallon's stomach. She murmured an incantation before she froze. Several moments passed before she moved again, and she smiled and stood. "You never cease to amaze me."

"Why? What did you see?" Fallon asked as she sat up.

Julianne looked at them with tears in her eyes before she said, "Two girls. Both witches… but one is a hybrid, like you, Fallon. A witch and a vampire. Both very powerful, but both will be set on very different paths"

Fallon's eyes grew wide as she asked, "Do we know them?"

Julianne's eyes sparkled before she nodded. "Everly…"

Fallon gasped as her hand went to her heart. Her mother… technically, Everly would always be her mother for an eternity because she had given birth to Fallon in her final lifetime. To think that she was being reborn again so soon… and to her… it was wild. Tears splashed out of her eyes as she asked, "And the other?"

"Lily," Julianne finished as a tear fell from her eye because she knew how much this would mean to Fallon.

Fallon's hands flew to her stomach as her throat tightened. She couldn't believe the powers that be had blessed her so abundantly. She no longer feared the work it would take to raise three magical beings. Instead, she couldn't wait for the inevitable reunion that was about to happen.

The End… For now!

Did you guys think I was really going to leave you hanging with Everly's story? Never that! Coming October, 2023! Stay tuned!

CYN'S CATALOG

Get signed copies at: Cynful Monarch

SERIES:

The Urban Fairytales Series (Complete Collection - all books in 1): https://amzn.to/2V7rk6d

Dust to Diamonds (Book 1 of the Urban Fairytale Series): https://amzn.to/3rT9srt

The Baddest of Them All (Book 2 of the Urban Fairytale Series): https://amzn.to/3lnnSyU

Lil Red Ryder (Book 3 of the Urban Fairytale Series): https://amzn.to/3xoLbKV

Rebel & Her Beast (Book 4 of the Urban Fairytale Series): https://amzn.to/3ih5kyr

A Fairytale Wedding (Book 5 of the Urban Fairytale Series): https://amzn.to/3rQ6O63

The Princess & the Goon (Spin-off of the Urban Fairytale Series): https://amzn.to/3fkDmQf

Billion Dollar Baddie: https://amzn.to/37cGVnr

Billion Dollar Baddie 2: https://amzn.to/3A4GRCm

Anything for the Family: https://amzn.to/3CcdvEi

Anything for the Family 2: https://amzn.to/3w0oqyt

Lux Rose: https://amzn.to/3wuib6e

Lux Rose 2: https://amzn.to/3MrZlCJ

Lux Rose 3: https://amzn.to/3Roq9re

Fang Gang: https://amzn.to/3C6PYFn

Fang Gang 2: https://amzn.to/3V9WTVL

STANDALONES:

Baby, it's Cold Outside: https://amzn.to/2V7ZSoX

The Married Woman: https://amzn.to/33k9jp1

A Hood Chick's Savior: https://amzn.to/3ykaAHf

Hell Hath No Fury: Beaten at your Own Game: https://amzn.to/3FmZRyE

LET'S CONNECT!

Join my readers group on Facebook, and stay up on
all releases, get character visuals and sneak peeks,
and even get in on giveaways!
https://www.facebook.com/groups/
277463019954112/

Hey There!

Thank you for your support on my literary
journey. I hope your reading experience was
a pleasant one. Please leave a review on
Goodreads and Amazon. Please feel free to
connect with me to stay current on upcoming
releases and reader specific exclusives.

www.ingramcontent.com/pod-product-compliance
Lightning Source LLC
Chambersburg PA
CBHW022141150726
47992CB00002B/701